ALSO BY ALEDA SHIRLEY

Long Distance (University of Miami Press, 1996)
Chinese Architecture (University of Georgia Press, 1986)

The Beach Book

A LITERARY COMPANION

Edited by

Aleda Shirley

SARABANDE  BOOKS

LOUISVILLE, KENTUCKY

Copyright © 1999 by Aleda Shirley

Cover painting: *September Magic*, by Rochelle Levy.
Reproduced by kind permission of the artist.

Cover and text design by Charles Casey Martin.

Manufactured in the United States of America.
This book is printed on acid-free paper.

Sarabande Books is a nonprofit literary organization.

LIBRARY OF CONGRESS CATALOGING-IN-PUBLICATION DATA

The beach book : a literary companion / edited by Aleda Shirley.
    p.   cm.
  ISBN 1-889330-27-2 (alk. paper)
  1. Beaches—Literary collections. 2. American literature—20th century.
I. Shirley, Aleda.
PS509.B38B43   1999
810.8'032146—dc21   98-34381
                                                    CIP

Contents

Introduction

Time spent at the beach doesn't feel quite like time spent inland; it elongates and widens; the days have a quality that is both more vivid and more blurred than that of normal days. Human beings are mostly made of water, and perhaps this explains the need so many people have to head to the edges of the continent in summer. Perhaps no other landscape evokes so much emotion as does the sea: grief and triumph, romance and loss, innocence and destruction. Even though as a child I lived for a time a few blocks from the ocean, I can still recall almost every time I have ever been to the beach, and I am confident I am not alone in this. I'm sure that every family or group of friends who goes to the beach establishes its own rituals and traditions and easy pace: a walk on the beach at dawn; gin and tonics at six; card games on rainy afternoons; bouillabaisse on the last night. Certainly my friends and I, after several holidays on the Gulf Coast of Florida, have come up with our own ways of doing things, our own private lexicon of jokes and references, our own shared history. Much of it exists in memory and conversation, but there are also photographs where I can see the house we stayed in the first summer, the bright yellow floats everyone bought one year, the red convertible one of us rented, the children (teenagers now) at seven and ten. We all look happy in those pictures (even those of us who dislike being photographed in swimsuits), and that, I think, is the point: people, more often than not, look happy when they are at the beach.

The Beach Book—the idea for it in its most embryonic form—

started when we were planning our second summer trip to the beach some years ago. I proposed we add a new activity: that during the cocktail hour we read something out loud to each other—something wonderful and magical, something somehow connected to the sea, perhaps Shakespeare, something, at any rate, that we wouldn't likely read for pleasure on our own.

The response to this was more enthusiastic than I had imagined it would be. In fact everyone was wild for the idea. And so we decided to read *The Tempest*, a play set on an island ruled by a magician, and my friend Mary Hartwell duly ordered eight copies of *The Tempest* from Square Books. Oxford, Mississippi, is a small town. While it isn't necessarily true that everyone is into everyone's business, it may be true that everyone is at least curious about everyone else's literary business, and the sight of all those paperback copies of a Shakespeare play in the special-order section behind the Square Books cash register prompted some questions.

When I went in to pick our books up, I ran into some friends. They had heard we were planning to read *The Tempest* aloud during our vacation. They looked wistful and almost envious: *That sounds like so much fun!* The woman behind the counter expressed a similar sentiment. I couldn't help but point out that everyone was free to read Shakespeare—or anything else—aloud at any time of the year; that while there was something decidedly delicious about doing it on a third-story deck overlooking the Gulf, it was also an activity one could pursue in one's own living room, in the dead of winter.

It got me thinking, the reaction to our plan.

We did indeed read *The Tempest* out loud that summer, at dusk, with our drinks sitting on the top rail of the deck and our legs propped up on the middle rail. Since it had been my idea, I insisted on being

Prospero. Our friend from Germany was a suitably tremulous Miranda. Someone else growled Caliban's part hilariously. There is a photograph from one of those evenings (we read one act a day), and when I look at it, everything comes back to me: the warm air and the salt breezes, a huge sky going indigo and pale orange before us, the clacking of the screen door and the difficult, magical language of the play.

A COUPLE OF MILES from Blue Mountain Beach in Florida is the town of Seaside, which has a small bookstore run by friends. Our summer vacations always include a trip there, to pick up a mystery, to check out the poetry section. What I noticed, in Sundog Books, was how different people seemed in that seaside bookstore than they did in ordinary bookstores; they seemed both avid and languorous as they picked up books off the tables and thumbed through them, as if their very proximity to the water somehow conjured up a longing for the written word and the process of reading. It is true that people at the beach have time on their hands, in a way they don't when they aren't on vacation, but that alone doesn't account for the ardent way in which they chose and discussed and bought stacks of shiny new books.

Many writers have said they started writing because they wanted to write the book they wanted to read but couldn't find. This is the anthology I would like to have at the beach, the book I want to give people going to the beach, the book I'd suggest to people looking for something fun and different and thought-provoking to read while stretched out on a sandy beach towel or relaxing on a screened porch—poems, stories, and essays that offer a new way of looking at the familiar, eternal place where the sea meets land.

—*Aleda Shirley*
Jackson, Mississippi

Jane Hirshfield

Just Below the Surface

Just below the surface, fish, still.
In the late afternoon, the sunlight ladders down,
breaking across their bodies' narrow poise.
It is almost a music, the brown unmoving quickness
intersected with gold.
They are, even in sleep, wholly alive and one, a necklace
assembled on thread so fine it is almost surmise.
A first moves, another, and they are gone.
As one lover goes, and, long after, the other;
yet somehow, in another shadow of the same water,
are still there.

Li-Young Lee
Water

The sound of 36 pines side by side surrounding
the yard and swaying all night like individual hymns is the sound
of water, which is the oldest sound,
the first sound we forgot.

At the ocean
my brother stands in water
to his knees, his chest bare, hard, his arms
thick and muscular. He is no swimmer.
In water
my sister is no longer
lonely. Her right leg is crooked and smaller
than her left, but she swims straight.
Her whole body is a glimmering fish.

Water is my father's life-sign.
Son of water who'll die by water,
the element which rules his life shall take it.
After being told so by a wise man in Shantung,

after almost drowning twice,
he avoided water. But the sign of water
is a flowing sign, going where its children go.

Water has invaded my father's
heart, swollen, heavy,
twice as large. Bloated
liver. Bloated legs.
The feet have become balloons.
A respirator mask makes him look
like a diver. When I lay my face
against his—the sound of water
returning.

The sound of washing
is the sound of sighing,
is the only sound
as I wash my father's feet—
those lonely twins
who have forgotten one another—
one by one in warm water
I tested with my wrist.
In soapy water
they're two dumb fish
whose eyes close in a filmy dream.

I dry, then powder them
with talc rising in clouds
like dust lifting

behind jeeps, a truck where he sat
bleeding through his socks.
1949, he's 30 years old,
his toenails pulled out,
his toes beaten a beautiful
violet that reminds him
of Hunan, barely morning
in the yard, and where
he walked, the grass springing back
damp and green.

The sound of rain
outlives us. I listen,
someone is whispering.
Tonight, it's water
the curtains resemble, water
drumming on the steel cellar door, water
we crossed to come to America,
water I'll cross to go back,
water which will kill my father.
The sac of water we live in.

Chase Twichell

Why All Good Music Is Sad

Before I knew that I would die,
I lolled in the cool green twilight
over the reef, the hot sun on my back,
watching the iridescent schools
flick and glide among stone flowers,
and the lacy fans blow back and forth
in the watery winds of the underworld.
I saw the long, bright muscle of a fish
writhing on a spear, spasm and flash,
a music violent and gleaming,
abandoned to its one desire.
The white radiance of Perdido
filtered down through the rocking gloom
so that it was Perdido there too,
in that strange, stroking, half-lit world.
Before I knew that love
would end my willful ignorance of death,
I didn't think there was much
left in me that was virgin, but there was.

That's why all good music is sad.
It makes the sound of the end before the end,
and leaves behind it
the ghost of the part that was sacrificed,
a chord to represent the membrane,
broken only once, that keeps the world away.
That's how the fish became the metaphor:
one lithe and silvery life impaled,
fighting death with its own failing beauty,
thrashing on the apex of its fear.
Art was once my cold solace,
the ice pack I held to love's torn body,
but that was before I lay
as if asleep above the wavering reef,
or saw the barbed spear strike the fish
that seemed for an instant to be
something outside myself, before I knew
that the sea was my bed and the fish was me.

Peter Cameron

Nuptials & Heathens

Joan is trying to decide if Tom's habit of switching the car radio from station to station is endearing or annoying. As they drive north of Boston, into the late night and away from the good stations, he punches the buttons more and more frequently. He is never satisfied with one station for long. They are driving to his parents' house in Maine for the weekend.

She rolls up her window because it is getting cold, and puts her empty Tab can on the floor at her feet, then picks it up because she's not sure it is something she should do in his car. When they stopped for gas she took fifty-five cents from the "toll money" (they were off the highway and through with tolls) and bought a Tab from the machine. When she tilted the can under Tom's chin for him to sip from, he said, "Ugh, Tab. Couldn't you have got a soda we both liked?"

TOM'S MOTHER, MRS. THORENSON, hears them arrive, but she doesn't get out of bed. She doesn't look so great in the middle of the night, and first impressions are first impressions. She listens to them come inside, hears them trying to be quiet, hears Tom pointing things out— "There's the ocean down there. See it?" She listens to them use the bathroom. It sounds like they're using it together—at least they're talking while Tom urinates (it sounds like a man urinating)—although Joan could be standing in the hall. Then she hears them go upstairs, together, into his room. She's glad she's not up to see that part. She hears them get into bed. She falls asleep listening for them to make love.

THE SUN DOESN'T WAKE JOAN UP. Tom does. "You better get up," he says. "We get up early here." He is standing by the bed in the pale blue tennis shorts she helped him pick out Thursday night in Herman's. Tom isn't tan, although it's August. From this angle, lying in bed with Tom standing beside her, the hair on his legs looks very unattractive. She gets out of bed and stands beside Tom in her Nike T-shirt.

"What should I wear?" she asks. "Do you get dressed up for breakfast?" When can I take a shower? she thinks to herself. Now, or after breakfast? Do they have a shower? She didn't see one in the bathroom last night.

"Not dressed up," says Tom. He pulls his matching blue-and-white-striped shirt over his head and speaks from inside it. "But dressed."

Joan looks out the window. A woman is dragging a black cat on a leash across the lawn. The cat looks dead.

"That's Deborah," says Tom. They both stand by the window and watch Deborah. "I don't know what that is she's got."

"It's a cat," says Joan.

"It looks like a skunk."

"Is your father here, too?" Joan asks. She puts on her jean skirt, then pulls off her T-shirt.

"I'm not sure," Tom says. "Let's hope not."

———

IN THE KITCHEN, Mrs. Thorenson is cutting up fruit for a fruit salad. She bought kiwifruit at The Fruit Basket just for this weekend, but she is unsure how to slice them. Should she peel them? The fuzzy skin looks unappetizing and vaguely dangerous. Yet, when she tries to peel them, the soft green flesh mushes up. She has, at Fanny Farmer's suggestion, quartered the strawberries, sliced (diagonally) the bananas, sectioned the grapefruit, and balled the cantaloupe with a teaspoon, but Fanny Farmer doesn't mention kiwifruit. The kiwis are hopeless. She throws them away. Good riddance to them, although at ninety-nine cents each it is a shame.

She watches Deborah tie her cat—what was its name, Gilda?—to the rail of the deck and come inside.

"Do you think it's safe to leave him out there?" Deborah asks.

"Of course," Mrs. Thorenson says. Gilbert climbs onto the canvas director's chair and lies in the sun. "Just make sure he doesn't fall off the deck and hang himself."

"He can't," says Deborah. She opens the refrigerator and looks in it. "He has on a harness, not a collar. Have they come down yet?"

"No," says Mrs. Thorenson. "But they're awake."

"She left her soap in the bathroom," Deborah says. "Clinique."

"So?" says Mrs. Thorenson.

"So, nothing. Just FYI."

THE MORNING GOES O.K. Mrs. Thorenson's fruit salad is a big hit, the coffee Deborah laced with cinnamon makes the kitchen smell nice, and Joan begins to relax. There is a shower, a nice one with a Water Pik showerhead and plenty of hot water, and after breakfast Joan takes a long shower and changes into her bathing suit.

They all sit on the deck for a while. Deborah lets Gilbert off the leash, and he sits in some bayberry bushes purring and looking dazed. At ten o'clock Mrs. Thorenson and Deborah drive to the airport to pick up Mr. Thorenson, who missed his flight the night before.

Joan and Tom go down to the beach. It's rocky except for one small area that's surrounded by railroad ties and filled with sand—bought sand, Tom explains, sand replaced every summer and after extremely high tides. They keep sacks of it in the boathouse.

But it's like a little oasis, and Tom and Joan lie on it, on an old bedspread that has a Wizard of Oz motif, only Dorothy doesn't look like Judy Garland, she looks like Heidi. She's blonde and dressed in lederhosen.

The blonde, skipping Dorothys unnerve Joan, but when she closes her eyes and traces the indentation down Tom's warm back again and again—a gesture she usually reserves for after they have made love—she begins to feel better, and by the time Deborah appears on the little beach, with Gilbert back on his leash, she's almost happy. It's not so bad here. It's nice.

"Daddy missed that plane, too," Deborah announces. "Mommy's beginning to get worried."

"Can't she call?" asks Tom. He doesn't open his eyes.

"She did. There's no answer." Deborah drops the leash and wades into the waves. Gilbert crouches on the beach looking terrified.

Joan sits up and watches Deborah in the water. When she was in college, Deborah was married to a Pakistani exchange student. Tom told Joan this, but also told her it is no longer mentioned. His exact words were "dead and buried."

"Have you been in the water yet?" Deborah calls.

"No," Joan shouts, "but I'm hot."

"Come in," Deborah shouts back. "It's great."

Joan gets up and steps over Gilbert, who flinches. She stands with her feet in the moist sand at the edge of the water, allowing the waves to come to her. She feels dizzy standing up.

Deborah splashes in toward shore, peels off her tank top and throws it on the beach. It lands near Gilbert, who bolts up the path toward the house. Deborah runs back out and dives under a wave. She has nothing on under the tank top.

"I forgot to take my contacts out," Joan says to no one: Deborah is underwater, and Tom doesn't hear her.

Deborah's head, brown shoulders, and white breasts slip out of the water, and she flings her hair back from her face. "Come on," she calls to Joan. "It's great."

"I have to take my contacts out," Joan yells. "I'll be right back."

Deborah makes some facial expression that Joan can't interpret: it could be irritation or sympathy or disgust.

Joan touches Tom's back with one of her wet toes, and says, for the third time in as many minutes, "I forgot to take my contacts out. Can I go up?"

"Sure," says Tom. "Would you bring down the suntan lotion? I think my shoulders are getting burned."

"They are," says Joan. "You better be careful. Turn over."

MRS. THORENSON IS SITTING on the deck under a huge lavender-and-white-striped umbrella, drinking orange juice.

"I'm sorry my husband is ruining your weekend," she says, as Joan comes up the path. Her sunglasses have a pink plastic triangle over the nose, which she has flipped up, so it looks like a tiny horn coming out from between her eyes.

Joan was not aware that Mr. Thorenson was ruining her weekend.

"Oh, hardly," she says, while she thinks about what she should say. "I'm having a good time."

"I'm not," says Mrs. Thorenson. "Maybe it would be better if he didn't come. Did Tom tell you he's found religion?"

Tom had mentioned something about Mr. Thorenson's newfound religious zeal, saying it was all because the doctors made him give up bridge, because he was getting "obsessive." But Joan isn't sure what this has to do with him missing all these planes: Is he one of those weirdos who try to sell flowers in airports? Surely he's not that bad.

Joan decides to play it safe and resorts to her now standard line. "I've come up to take my contact lenses out," she says. "I'm going in for a swim."

Mrs. Thorenson takes a sip of her drink. An ice cube falls out of the glass and onto the wooden deck, where it quickly begins melting in the sun. The melting ice cube reminds Joan of the speedup movies she used to see of crocuses blooming, only in reverse.

"I didn't know you wore contacts," Mrs. Thorenson says.

"Yes," Joan says. "For years."

"Come here," says Mrs. Thorenson. "Let me see." She reaches out her tanned hand and motions Joan over. "Are they hard or soft?"

"Hard," says Joan. She bends down and lets Mrs. Thorenson hold her chin and turn her face sideways. She opens her eyes wide. She's looking at a wooden sign nailed to the side of the house that says WELCOME SHIPMATES.

"So you do," says Mrs. Thorenson. Her hot breath lands on Joan's cheek. There is more than juice in that glass, Joan thinks.

BEFORE JOAN RETURNS, Deborah gets out of the water and puts her tank top back on. "Where's Gilbert?"

Tom sits up. "He ran up to the house. I don't think he liked it down here."

"Do you like Gilbert?" asks Deborah. She sits down on the bedspread where Joan had been lying, forming a big wet spot.

"He's all right," says Tom. "I don't know."

"You could at least cheer up a little," says Deborah. She puts on her punk sunglasses. "What's the matter?"

"Nothing," says Tom. "Let me try them on."

Deborah gives him the sunglasses. He tries them on. They do things for him. "They look great," says Deborah. She reaches over and takes them off. "But they look greater on me."

"Do you like Joan?" asks Tom.

"Why?" asks Deborah. "Are you going to marry her?"

"I'm going to ask her," Tom says.

"Seriously?" says Deborah. "You're kidding."

"No," says Tom. "I'm serious. At least about asking her."

"I can't believe it," says Deborah. "I thought you just met her."

"At Christmas," Tom says. "Last Christmas." He lies back down. "It's summer now," he says as if it just dawned on him.

"When are you going to ask her?" says Deborah. "I want to watch."

"I'm not sure," says Tom. "Sometime this weekend. When the moment is right."

"Jesus Christ," says Deborah. "I can't believe you're going to get married."

"But do you like her?"

Before Deborah can answer, Joan stumbles onto the beach. "I can't see anything," she says. "Where's the water?"

AFTER LUNCH MRS. THORENSON has Tom hold the ladder while she ties TV dinner trays to the cherry tree. Their clatter and reflection scare the birds away. Mrs. Thorenson went out and bought ten macaroni-and-cheese TV dinners (the cheapest) before she realized she could have used aluminum pie plates. The women's magazine had recommended the TV dinner trays, instead of just throwing them away. Mrs. Thorenson doesn't really like cherries—they have pits—but it bothers her that the birds get them. The sea gulls are always sitting fatly under the tree, their breasts stained red.

Joan is sitting on the ground shucking corn for dinner. Some of the silk is picked up and carried off by the breeze, and it hangs like lighted hair in the air. Joan watches it disappear into the pine trees.

Mrs. Thorenson's head is hidden by leaves and TV dinner trays, but Joan is listening to her talk. "I wish this were a peach tree. Wouldn't it be nice if this were a peach tree? This tree was a gift from a woman I never liked. She stayed here one weekend when we first built the house and she gave us this cherry tree as a house gift. I don't remember how it got planted. I remember it sat in a burlap bag for a long time after she left.

"That was back when Daddy came up on the seaplane with Mr. Thomas Friday nights and landed on Great Snake Pond. Do you remember? We'd go over there after dinner and wait on the dock and you and Deborah would have flashlights—it would just be getting dark. And the plane would appear and get closer and closer and land with a splash and Daddy would get out on the dock in his business suit, holding his briefcase, dropped from the sky. Do you remember?"

"No," says Tom. "I must have repressed it."

"Why would you have repressed it?" Mrs. Thorenson asks. A TV dinner tray falls out of the tree.

"I don't know," says Tom. "Maybe it was painful."

"You were probably just too young," Mrs. Thorenson says. "Maybe Deborah remembers. Deborah must."

Tom looks over to see if Joan is watching, and when he sees she is, he mimes kicking the ladder out from under Mrs. Thorenson. Tom is sulking because his shoulders are sunburned. Tom is a sulker, Joan is realizing. When they changed out of their bathing suits, Tom noticed the red streaks beginning to bloom across his white shoulders. He blamed Joan, accusing her of not applying the sunblock properly. As he stands under the tree, he keeps craning his neck to get a better view of his back.

Joan watches, amused, but there's something about the leafy pattern of shadows moving across Tom's mottled skin that makes him look a little leprous from behind. This thought nauseates her, so she concentrates on the corn. When she first met Tom at her old boyfriend's Christmas party, she thought he was wonderful. He was very good-looking, and a great, tireless dancer, and after the party he insisted they go out for breakfast. On their way home in the cab, Tom shot the stoplights from red to green, and he hit every one, and as the cab flew down the deserted avenue, Joan began to think she might be falling in love. It was very magical. But the next morning she worried it might have been the wicked punch. And ever since it's followed that pattern: Tom will do something nice—buy her flowers, make love to her especially well, invite her to Maine—something that will intoxicate her, but then a few minutes or hours or days later she'll lose interest in him again. One of the reasons she came to Maine was to get a grip on all this and decide one way or another. She pulls the silk off the last ear of corn. She feels lightheaded, but it's not the wine she is drinking that makes her feel giddy. It's something else.

What is it? Joan thinks. Then she realizes. It's because she knows she doesn't love Tom. All these months she has been trying to convince herself otherwise. But now—right now—she knows. As she stuffs the last strands of corn silk into the brown paper bag she feels truly out of love with Tom. Everything will change now, she has a feeling, everything will be all right. She laughs. She can't help it.

"What are you laughing at?" asks Tom.

"Nothing," says Joan. "I'm just happy."

"Are you?" says Tom. He smiles. "So am I."

AT DINNER, at a restaurant called Oysters & Oxes, Tom asks Joan to marry him. The waiter arrives with a bottle of champagne Tom secretly ordered on a trip to the men's room, and the whole uncorking procedure gives Joan some time to think about how she should say no.

Then the waiter is gone, and she's left with Tom sitting across from her, a glass of champagne raised in front of him, repeating his embarrassing proposal. Joan's champagne glass is still on the table and she can feel the bubbly mist cooling her throat.

Tom's serious face glowing sincerely in the candlelight makes her feel sad and guilty. How could she have let things go this far? This is a predicament she associates with movies—old movies—or with her mother's time.

"Marry?" she says, as if it's a word with many shades of meaning.

"Yes," says Tom. "Don't you think we should?"

"No," says Joan.

Tom puts down his champagne glass. "Oh," he says. He picks it up again and drinks from it.

Joan thinks, This is so wrong. She's sure that all the people she knows who are married decided mutually while watching TV or baking bread or wallpapering their apartments. She and Tom do none of these things. They go to the movies and out to dinner once or twice a week and sleep together on the weekends, but they've never been through anything together or gone on a trip or even had a big fight. It's just not a serious relationship. Why doesn't Tom know this? It's scary to think that he can be in love with her on the basis of so little.

She excuses herself and goes down to the women's room. There is a hand-lettered sign that looks like an invitation taped to the mirror, explaining that, since the women's room is below sea level, please don't flush tampons down the toilet.

When she comes back the mussels have disappeared. She drinks some champagne. "I'm sorry," she says. "You surprised me."

"It's O.K.," says Tom. "We can talk about it later."

She should tell him no, never, but she doesn't. She just smiles. "It was very nice of you," she says. "Thank you."

Tom shrugs. He is playing with the champagne cork, making it roll on the table in little lopsided circles. Joan thinks, If I said yes, he'd keep the cork as a souvenir, and every year on the anniversary of this date, he'd bring it out and show it to me.

WHEN THEY GET BACK to the house Deborah is standing in the sandy driveway. It is windy and the wind seems to blow even the stars around in the sky. Joan is a little drunk.

"Gilbert got away," Deborah announces, as they get out of the car. "I can't find him."

This domestic tragedy immediately cheers Joan; it's a welcome relief from the silent tension between her and Tom. The wind is waking her up, too.

"Gil-bert!" Joan shouts into the blowing bushes.

PETER CAMERON | 31

"I thought I could hear him meowing," Deborah says, "but I can't tell where it's coming from."

They all listen for a minute, but they don't hear Gilbert. Deborah shines her flashlight into the scrubby pine trees. Joan sits on the hood of the car and takes her shoes off. The tops of her feet are sunburnt. "Maybe he's down by the water," she says.

"Maybe he's dead," Tom says.

"I'm going to go look on the beach," Joan says, partly because she wants to see the water at night, partly because she wants to get away by herself. She gives Tom a look she hopes discourages him from joining her.

"Do you want a flashlight?" asks Deborah. "There's another one in the drawer beneath the breadbox."

"No," says Joan. She hops off the car. "It's bright out." She's right: the moon and the stars seem to be unusually—and unnervingly—near, as if they've dropped out of their niches and are falling.

"I'm going to go look over by Cooke's," says Deborah. "There was a dead rabbit over there last weekend Gilbert might have smelled. Come with me," she says to Tom. "I'm scared."

She and Tom walk down the driveway, across the dirt road, and into the woods. Deborah shines the flashlight at the ground; toadstools poke through the matted pine needles, forming little tents.

"So?" says Deborah.

"So, what?"

"So did you ask her?"

"Yes," says Tom. He kicks a toadstool and watches the white floweret fly through the air out of their circle of light. "She said no."

"Oh," says Deborah.

Tom stops walking and leans against a pine tree. He picks some lichen off the bark.

Deborah shines the flashlight at his face. "Are you sad?" she asks.

Tom looks at her, but can't see, because of the bright light in his eyes. "A little," he says. "I don't know."

"I wouldn't be too sad," says Deborah. "She seems like kind of a pill to me."

"Oh," says Tom.

"I mean, I'm sure she's nice. Are you really O.K.?"

"I'm O.K.," says Tom. "I just feel like a fool."

Deborah turns her flashlight off. "Gilbert's not really lost," she says. "I just made that up so I could get you away."

"Did Daddy come?"

"No," says Deborah. "But he called. From Dallas. He said there are a lot of heathens in Dallas."

"There are heathens everywhere," says Tom. "I'm a heathen."

"Don't tell Daddy that," Deborah says. She laughs.

"Where is Gilbert?"

"In my room."

"Maybe Joan will get lost looking for him," says Tom. "Maybe she'll never come back."

"Maybe," says Deborah.

JOAN WALKS AROUND THE HOUSE and onto the croquet lawn. The wickets grow out of the ground like strange curving reeds. Everything looks different, Joan thinks, when you're drunk and it's dark and windy and your life is changing. All she wants to do is get back to the city and start over again. She's already forgotten about Gilbert.

As she walks down the sloping field of wickets, something catches her eye on the other side of the house—the cherry tree. It's blowing in the wind and looks as if it's trying to shake the TV dinner trays off its limbs, and as Joan watches, one does come off, and sails, gleaming, into the night.

Kathleen Halme

Where the Cape Fear Empties into Ocean

In last week's big weather the ocean ate
the gazebo at the fat beach.
Sunday again, they're back:
the fast-food families, staking
claims in swimsuits big as sails.

Plant that cooler of salt snacks and fizz.
Stick that watermelon umbrella
on your little edge of ocean. In the shifting
continental drift of cellulose
we all want the primal dip.

Already a boy has found a baby shark.
He walks it like a clarinet, its jaw
a squeaking reed. The little primate
sneaks behind beached sleepers,
and plays the shark at their butts.

It's too soon to make a fuss:
we're a bit crabby this morning.
I grow nails and teeth,
unroll below the sea oats, and run
with my real husband into ocean.

Can you still touch? Yes, can you?
we ask until everyone in water
has dissolved below the shoulders.
Above us all, a whalish blimp chubs by
to tell us where to eat tonight.

Below us all,
the bottom dips
down in drift and
we're afloat with
plankton in the neaptide.

Bolted into hunger
we can't fight,
the current floats
us soaked with water.
We can't see

the larval mollusks,
the small sea cucumbers,
invisible to the naked
eye, drifting in
our extraneous suits.

We are in the soup, singular
and swimming, roiling
with the isopods and copepods.
We are motile, every one
of us buoyant

as bubbles
in the tidal cycle. Who can see
our feet kicking
over a great heart
cockle pumping water

into gills, over bulging
ark shells straining
plankton? We are delicious,
surrendered to shells and jellies,
every one soaking in sun.

Lilies Showering Down

I

On that island, I was learning what I loved:
a little life for an animal with eggs.
Clean as a peppermint, I gave off light!

I was slow as soap, my simplicity astounding.
Consider how infinite I was,
walking every inch of that orchid-shaped island:

no jangled thoughts, I knew only elegances:
a storm's wash pinks the beach with jellyfish;
in the salt marsh, visible in water,

a seahorse, small as a baby's finger,
wraps its tail around a reed to stay in place,
or possibly, for pleasure.

II

From way out in the ocean, he came
like a rower, pulling himself in wood
all the way to me.

He loved salt: three-hundred-year-
old meat, the block, the fingertip.
My lips were salt air sea.

I thought: hummingbird.
Miraculous verb, one could be
drawn to land on his salted palm.

Am I at all mysterious to you? he asked.
The blue notion fumed
until it flickered open utterly.

He gave and gave,
then led me close to trumpets
thread on devil's green;

I went under as the open sun
vined up the old snake shack
high at the rim of the sea.

      III

Below the fathers drape their mended nets to dry,
the mothers hang bleached
white by white and blue by blue.

I eat provisions I've collected for confinement:
jewel box of fish, a fist of soda bread,
some licorice pipes—black and undeniable.

I sleep alone on the circumference.
These lighthouse walls are five feet thick.
In hurricanes, a town could hide inside,
but this storm abides with me.

Equipoise

I could build a wild bonfire
above the sea to get you
to notice me, but
I like the nearness
to an everywhere of light.
I'm not hiding; this
is where I work, I live:
a lightning whelk, room
on top of room,
spired to the top.

I like the little
implements of ritual,
how separate prisms
polished in the morning
gather a hive of light
at dusk and fling it
at the white fold of horizon.

This is no tower of myth.
I can't wear old clothes
of lonely keepers,
who dipped the last

cup of sunset
to keep the lamps alive.

We all live in fear
of shoreless feelings,
but inside
this giant spark plug
as sumptuous as grace,
I see freshwater
freighters and saltwater
freighters floating
loads toward home.

David Wojahn

Shadow Girl

Below, the concrete bayou water leaps
along its strictures as I walk. Sunset,
and the joggers sway in profile against
the sky and onyx high-rise lights of Houston.
Side by side the next-door couple sprints
above the levee, flaunting their expensive
bodies, muscles rippling, oblivious grins
of self-regard. Sleek with perspiration,
they'll undress and make love in a dark

apartment, displaying their usual
shrill expertise. But later, the woman
will gaze awhile at the star quilt's clumsy
firmament, clothes flung like planets, straddling
the bed. How did she reach this place? I know
her longing can't be spoken. Call it secrecy,
neither recollection nor nostalgia.
Her husband twists and calls from sleep
robbing the air she breathes. She'll gaze

like this for hours. Last night in the airport's
strident fluorescent light, I watched your plane
climb east through clouds, our year-long separation
at midpoint now. I write tonight beyond
the muffled cries next door, remembering how
we strolled last year along the beaches
that composed your childhood, the creaking
boardwalk—amusement park shuttered for the season.
It reminded you of the final summer

before the Salk vaccine. July in New Jersey,
the beaches empty. Before sleep, you'd hear
the roller coaster's humming yellow scaffold
bulbs, the carousel silently revolving
its riderless horses. You were trying
to retrieve the smallest details of
those nights, the salt-air smell, the lighthouse arc
above you. Tonight, I know again how helplessly
we circle these separate childhoods,

sharing only marriage and the few
common gestures that the years have given,
how nights without you I wake to absence
almost palpable, how nights beside you
it's otherness I wake to, a secrecy
only partly mine, how marriage is
a pact with memory beyond ourselves.
It was twenty years ago: sure your parents
were asleep, you'd rise from the beach house cot,

unhinge the screen door hook, and walk all night
along the empty boardwalk. In the darkened
hall of mirrors you'd watch your vapory form,
afraid you were composed of only shadow,
a girl dancing feverish Ginger Rogers to prove
this image of herself could tell her something
magical. The girl picks up a shell and spins
its frail star in her hands. And in the mirror
the shadow girl answers back.

Jennifer Ackerman

Osprey

The temperature this morning is 82 degrees. The relative humidity is 85 percent. The wind is all by the sea; here in the bay it is quiet and warm. I've come to the cape in the hopes of seeing a pair of osprey, newly mated and nesting on a wooden platform by the bay. But the birds are nowhere in sight. Instead I spot a photographer in a three-piece suit, and his subjects, a groom in tails and a bride in a starchy white, high-necked gown. It is a pretty scene: Behind the pair, dunes stretch to the sea, patchy mats of beach heather exploding with the yellow bloom of May. But the bride seems annoyed. Her satin pumps fight the avalanching dunes, heels probing the sand like the bill of a willet. She reaches out to the groom to steady herself, removes a shoe, and empties a long stream of grit. She looks young, barely twenty. Beads of sweat soak the lace rimming her veil. The flies are up; the warm air carries the stench of creatures rotting on the flats.

Yesterday I was lucky enough to catch the ospreys copulating. Through my scope I could see the female in intimate detail perched on the edge of the platform, her glistening yellow eyes, the dusky shafts of her breastband, the soft green-gray of her feet. Her mate circled above, white belly shining in the sun. He whistled piercing notes, then dropped suddenly, dipping below the platform and swooping up to hover directly above her. He settled on her back gently, barely touching her with clenched talons, flapping his wings for balance. She tipped forward slightly, raising her tail high to the side to receive him. I watched, a little ashamed of my magnified view. They coupled in silence for twenty or thirty seconds. Then the female, with a light flutter of wings, shrugged off her mate, who slowly banked upward and slipped sidewise across the sky.

The osprey leapt into my heart from my first days here. For one thing, the big bird is easy to identify. So many shorebirds are what ornithologists call "LBJs," little brown jobs. These I tried to pin down in my notes with some vague hope of identifying them later. But the osprey's size, its white belly and dark carpal patches, its wings kinked at the wrist, gave it away. So did its slow whistled call, a penetrating *kyew, kyew,* which drifts down from overhead. I occasionally mistook a high-flying osprey for a gull, but eventually learned to read its pattern of flight: shallow wingbeats interspersed with long glides. Its movement was more purposeful and deliberate than a gull's, less flighty. The osprey's huge nests, most of them in open, public places, and its showy method of hunting—a dazzling power dive ending in a burst of spray—made it a conspicuous neighbor, familiar and expected.

WHEN I WAS SEVEN OR EIGHT I went bird-watching with my father from time to time. I remember rising before dawn reluctantly and heading out, stiff, sleepy, my shoes damp with dew. In a family of five girls, time alone with my dad was a rare pleasure, not to be missed. The two of us would feel our way along the towpath between the C & O Canal and the Potomac River, cool breeze on the backs of our necks, companionable in late starlight. We moved quietly, all eyes for the small woodland birds we hoped to spy from a distance. It would begin with one bird, maybe two, chipping away at the dark. Then the clear whistled note of a cardinal would rise and the trilling of a wood thrush, and the songs would pass from one bird to another, their swelling sounds lifting me up by my ears. As the stars faded and branches emerged against the sky, sudden small shapes would appear and disappear, fluttering and darting about, flashing between the leaves: sparrows, finches, warblers, which I could just barely make out in the darkness. I didn't try to identify them. At that hour the world was theirs. On the ride home in the car, I would sift through my father's well-thumbed volume of Roger Tory Peterson's *Field Guide to North American Birds*, neatly indexed with plastic tabs marking the division of families: *Paridae* (titmice), *Sittidae* (nuthatches), *Troglodytidae* (wrens), and *Parulidae* (wood warblers). I was a pushover for the neat little manual, a fine tool for thinking about diversity and order in the world.

What birds I saw on those excursions were mostly woodland species. When it came to shorebirds I was utterly lost. Some species were easy to pin down. The ruddy turnstone, for instance—a squat, aggressive little bird with a harlequin mask—or the black-bellied plover, with its long, elegant black bib. But the sandpipers were a different story. Peterson calls the littlest ones "peeps," the white-rumped, the semipalmated, the least. There are rules, of course— the least is the smallest, its diminutive size earning it the species name *minutilla;* the semipalmated has a shorter, stouter bill—but judging either bill or body size at a distance seemed hopeless. Then there was the matter of plumage, which changes from season to season like foliage and which differs from male to female, from juvenile to immature to adult. Same bird, different disguises. No sooner had I nailed down the various appearances of one migratory species than another had taken its place. It's no wonder Aristotle came up with the theory of transmutation: Birds change species with the season, he said. Redstarts, common in Greece throughout the summer, became robins in winter; summer garden warblers changed into winter blackcaps. He claimed to have seen the birds midway in their metamorphoses. Anyone who has tried to identify fall birds in their shabby molting plumage can understand the mistake.

I eventually found a tutor in Bill Frech, a kind, owlish man, now eighty, who has been a devoted observer of winged things since he was twelve. Bill is up and away every morning at dawn to make his rounds in a VW with a scope mounted on the window. Though he claims not to have any special knowledge of winds or weather, he knows where the birds will be on any particular day, where heavy rains form pools of standing water that draw glossy ibises and egrets, which hayfields have been cut over recently, making good habitat for golden plovers, which buoys offer refuge to storm petrels in heavy wind. He sees what he sees, he says, and a good part of his pleasure is in the chanciness of the enterprise. One morning might yield nothing more interesting than a common goldeneye or an upland plover, while the next turns up a stray swallow-tailed kite hovering over the Lewes water tower, an Australian silver gull, or two thousand gannets riding out a storm behind Hen and Chickens Shoal.

Bill sees the world of light and motion not in a continuum, he says, but in frozen frames, a series of discernible stopwatch tableaux, which helps him spot his quarry. He scours the edges of the land, the broad sweep of sky and sea, one section at a time, and nearly always turns up a bird. I have tried to learn to do this, to look for spots of stillness on the tossing sea, for movement among the stubble of a cut field, but I often miss the mark and must have my eye directed. Bill carries no field guides. He depends less on fieldmarks to identify a bird than on its jizz, a term that comes from the fighter pilot's acronym GIS for General Impression and Shape. He has taught me to recognize a semipalmated plover or to distinguish a yellowlegs from a willet without quite knowing how I do so, just as one recognizes a friend from a distance not by individual characteristics, but by shape and gait. Most sandpipers walk and probe, while the plover runs and pecks, runs and pecks. Spotted sandpipers teeter. The Maliseet Indians of Maine understood this. They called the bird *nan a-mik-tcus*, or "rocks its rump." The sanderling flies steadily along; the plover's flight is wilder, full of tilting twists and turns. Most warblers dart through trees, but myrtle warblers drift. Knowing the jizz of a bird is especially useful when it comes to identifying high-flying species: Canada geese flap constantly; cormorants glide, long black necks in eternal pursuit of tiny tufted heads; gannets dip like goldfinches; pelicans alternate flaps with a short sail. As Bill filled my head with these rules of thumb, the species slowly separated and gained names.

I HAVE THE GOOD FORTUNE to live within a three-mile radius of five active osprey nests. One sits atop a platform on the double cross-arms of an old utility pole in the marsh at the center of town, hard by a railroad and King's Highway. The highway carries the crush of traffic disgorged from the Cape May–Lewes ferry, a steady stream of tourists hell-bent for a seaward peep. Another nest occupies a channel marker, a fancy site complete with a flashing red light powered by a solar panel and two bright orange warning signs. The rest sit on duck blinds and man-made platforms. The ospreys seem unbothered by all the human activity surrounding these sites. They are adaptable, versatile sorts, with a predilection for human ruins. An unkempt chimney, a vacant house, or a pile of fence rails gone back to nature draws them in. On an island in the Chesapeake Bay that was once a bombing range, ospreys nest on the busted-up car bodies used as targets. One pair set up housekeeping on the surface of an unexploded thousand-pound bomb.

Every year, within a day or two of St. Patrick's Day, as schooling fish move into the sun-warmed waters of the bay, the ospreys arrive on the south wind for the breeding season. They fly in high and circle overhead, greeting each mudbank, each twist of creek with a high, clear whistle. Invariably a notice appears in the local paper: "The fish hawk, Delaware's harbinger of spring, has finally arrived."

The spectacle of courtship follows soon after. The young male selects a nesting site and then begins an aerial display, a slow, undulating flight high in the sky. Once an understanding is struck between a male of good property and his discriminating partner, nest building begins. The pair is up and down, in and out all day, scouring the neighborhood for appropriate materials. Ospreys are pack rats and indefatigable renovators. Though they nest in the same site from year to year, the nests themselves are often destroyed between seasons and so need considerable repairs. The birds don't seem particularly interested in permanence or stability. John Muir purportedly rode out a hurricane sitting on an eagle's nest. Ornithologist Alan Poole said he wouldn't trust his weight to an osprey nest on a blue windless day. At the nest near King's Highway, I've watched males bring in cornstalks, cow dung, crab shells, a fertilizer bag, a toy shovel, a slice of floor mat, and the doilylike remnants of fish net. Even this eclectic nest doesn't hold a candle to one John Steinbeck found in his Long Island garden, which contained three shirts, a bath towel, an arrow, and a rake.

The male plays hod carrier to the female's bricklayer. She has definite ideas about how things should be arranged and fulfills her task with zeal. The loose mass grows up and out until it looms like a giant mushroom cap against the horizon. Nest finished, the female turns broody, sitting deep in the nest cup so that only her head shows. The male brings her fish and often spells her while she perches nearby and consumes her meal head first, with a kind of horrible delicacy.

When I'm at a loss to explain some bit of bird biology or behavior I've observed, I turn to Arthur Cleveland Bent's mighty twenty-volume series on the *Life Histories of North American Birds.* (Bill Frech started acquiring copies of the books in the 1920s, when the U.S. Government Printing Office sent them out free. He got all but the last three volumes, which he had to buy from the publisher.) The organization of these volumes is tidy and pleasing. The section on ospreys, for instance, lists the bird's full Latin name, *Pandion haliaëtus carolinensis.* Then the common name, from the Latin *ossifraga,* or sea eagle. Then come sections filled with copious details on courtship, nesting, plumage, voice, enemies, and eggs, all enhanced by the observations of a large company of tipsters. Here's Mr. Clinton G. Abbott's catalogue of osprey calls:

> The commonest note is a shrill whistle, with a rising inflection: *Whew, whew, whew, whew, whew, whew, whew.* This is the sound usually heard during migration; and when the bird is only slightly aroused. When she becomes thoroughly alarmed it will be: *Chick, chick, chick, cheek, cheek, ch-cheek, ch-cheek, cheereek, chezeek, chezeek,* gradually increasing to a frenzy of excitement at the last. Another cry sounds like: *Tseep, tseep, tseep-whick, whick, whick-ick-ick-ck-ck,* dying away in a mere hiccough.

It is no easy task to record bird sound on paper, and you have to admire the efforts of Abbott. One crochety contributor expresses disappointment in this range: "All these notes . . . seem inadequate to express the emotions of so large a bird."

For the latest field studies on ospreys, I turn to Alan Poole's book, *Ospreys: A Natural and Unnatural History*. Here are hundreds of businesslike facts: the number of minutes of hunting necessary to meet the daily food requirements of an osprey family (195), the percentage of eggs lost from an average clutch in New York (68%) and in Corsica (21%), the total population of breeding pairs in Britain (45) and along the Chesapeake Bay (1,500).

According to both Bent and Poole, ospreys are traditional, one could even say conservative, birds. A female selects her mate not by his fancy flight, melodious song, or flamboyant feathers, but by his choice of homes. The birds favor the top limbs of large, mature, isolated trees. In a typical old-growth forest, fewer than one in a thousand trees suit. On this coast, where mature forests are mostly gone, the birds resort to distinctly unnatural sites: telephone poles, channel markers, fishing piers, and duck blinds. They favor overwater sites, which offer good protection from raccoons and other four-footed predators, but are of no use against winged carnivores such as the great horned owl. I've seen these formidable hunters perched on the Lewes water tower, heard them caterwauling in the dark, and found their pellets in the pine forest, packed solid with bones, feathers, and fur.

Ospreys are thought to mate for life. However, a recent story in *The New York Times* tells me that there is almost no such thing as true monogamy in the animal kingdom. It reports that scientists are uncovering evidence of philandering in species after species, withering the notion of lovingly coupled birds. With sophisticated spying techniques, they are spotting members of supposedly faithful pairs—purple martins, barn swallows, black-capped chickadees—flitting off for extramarital affairs. With DNA fingerprinting, they've compiled dossiers on the adulterers. One of the few known examples of true monogamy, they say, is a rodent living in the weeds and grasses of the midwestern prairies, a homely little vole called *Microtus ochrogaster*, which is utterly committed to its mate.

Still, it is fairly well established that adultery is rare among ospreys, and there are stories of fervent conjugal devotion. Bent reports the story of a bird whose mate was killed when a bolt of lightning struck her nest. The male refused to abandon the site, perching in a nearby tree all summer, a bird-shaped picture of bereavement. He returned the following year and stood vigil for another season.

A typical osprey clutch consists of three eggs, which Bent describes as "the handsomest of all the hawks' eggs...roughly the size of a hen's egg." Bent collected eggs most of his life, saved the orbs as trophies, laying their speckles in a cabinet fragrant with that peculiar pungent egg odor. "I shall never forget my envious enthusiasm," he writes, "when a rival boy collector showed me the first fish hawk's eggs I had ever seen." He goes on to describe the range of their appearance in loving detail: "The shell is fairly smooth and finely granulated. The ground color...may be white, creamy white, pinkish white, pale pinkish cinnamon, fawn color, light pinkish cinnamon, or vinaceous-cinnamon. They are usually heavily blotched and spotted with dark rich browns or bright reddish browns, bone brown, liver brown, bay, chestnut, burnt sienna, or various shades of brownish drab."

It was after reading this description that I bought a scope to watch more closely the activities of the ospreys nesting near King's Highway.

I couldn't see the eggs themselves: They sat too low in the nest. But sometime late in the second week of June, they hatched. The newborn chicks were unfinished things, fuzzy flesh poking up from the bottom of the nest, as naked and helpless as a human baby, and no less perishably tender. Unlike such precocial birds as plovers and sandpipers, which go forth into the world straight from the egg, young ospreys take some coddling. Despite a steady stream of fish delivered by its parents, one chick died ten days later. The survivor, a fat squab with golden pinfeathers and thick black eye stripes, turned mobile at about four weeks, pestering its mother for fish and backing up now and again to squirt feces over the nest's edge. By midsummer, fatted on shad and flounder, puffed up on menhaden, it was flapping its scrawny wings, testing flight.

One warm, still day later that summer, I watched a young osprey fishing in the bay. The water was alive with hundreds of small silver fish that split the calm, sun-smooth surface. The bird flew in high from the southwest, slowly spiraled down to seventy or eighty feet, and began to stalk the shallows. The bright eye opened, the head lowered, the wings folded, then the feet thrust forward and the bird dropped like a feathered bomb, striking the water with a burst of spray.

Millions of generations of natural selection have made these birds good at what they do. Though ospreys have been known to take snakes, turtles, voles, and even baby alligators, 99 percent of their diet is fish, and they play every piscine angle. They spot fish from hundreds of feet above the water, even bottom fish with superb camouflage, like flounder. They penetrate the sun's glare or a dark, rippled water surface and adjust their strike to compensate for light refraction. With an eye membrane called a pecten, they change focus instantly to keep the fish in perfect view as they plunge. They hit the water at speeds of twenty to forty miles per hour. Their dense, compact plumage protects against the force of the impact; a flap of tissue on top of the beak closes over the nostrils to shut out the splash. The bird's strong, sinewy legs are superbly adapted for catching and holding slippery prey. Sharp talons, curved and of equal length, can snap shut in a fiftieth of a second. One toe swings back so that the osprey can clutch its prey with two claws on either side. Short spines on the base of the bird's toes and footpads ensure a firm grip.

With several deep wingbeats, this young bird rose slowly, shook its wings, and shifted the wildly flapping quiver of silver in its broad talons so that it rode headfirst, like a rudder. I watched until nothing could be seen of it but the dark V-sign of wings against the sky.

ALDO LEOPOLD ONCE WROTE about the physics of beauty in the sand hills of Wisconsin. "Everybody knows . . . that the autumn landscape in the north woods is the land, plus a red maple, plus a ruffed grouse. In terms of conventional physics, the grouse represents only a millionth of either the mass or the energy of an acre. Yet subtract the grouse and the whole thing is dead. . . . A philosopher has called this imponderable essence the *numenon* of material things." For me, the osprey supplies the same kind of motive power to this place.

In the 1950s and '60s, this coast nearly lost its numenon to DDT, what Rachel Carson called the "elixir of death." March brought few homecomers, June grew no aerie. The toxic brew did more damage to the osprey than had been done by decades of egg collecting, hunting, and habitat destruction.

During World War II, the U.S. Army had used DDT to combat body lice among its troops, successfully breaking the chain of typhus infection. After the war, farmers and government workers began using the pesticide as a weapon against mosquitoes and agricultural pests. Its hazards were recognized from the beginning. Two researchers from the U.S. Fish and Wildlife Service published a paper in 1946 warning of the dangers of DDT. They had found that spraying in New Jersey endangered blue crabs. In Pennsylvania, it was brook trout; in Maryland, birds, frogs, toads, snakes, and fish. Still, for almost three decades, most of the East Coast's shoreline and marshes were blanketed with DDT in an effort to eradicate the common salt-marsh mosquito. Long-lasting and easily dispersed, the pesticide spread over the earth in much the same pattern as radioactive fallout, carried aloft by wind and deposited on the ground in rainfall. By the 1960s, it permeated wildlife all around the globe, even lodging in tissues of Adélie penguins in Antarctica.

The highest concentrations of DDT residues were found in carnivorous birds at the top of the food chain: bald eagles, peregrine falcons, ospreys. The pesticide found its way into plankton and phytoplankton (microscopic plants and algae such as diatoms and dinoflagellates), which were eaten by shellfish, insects, and other creatures, which were eaten by fingerlings, which were in turn eaten by larger fish, which were caught by osprey. The concentration of the pesticide increased as much as ten times with each level in the chain. (Fish also accumulate toxins by absorbing pollutants directly through their gills.) What started out as a minute amount of DDT in water or plants ended up as a big dose in fish and an even bigger dose in the fatty tissues of birds of prey.

Ospreys can rid themselves of small amounts of some toxins: mercury, for instance. They excrete it from the blood into growing feathers, which are eventually molted—a technique that works only during the molting season. But mercury occurs in nature; DDT is man-made. Birds have had no time to evolve a way to rid their bodies of the poison. As the toxin accumulates in fatty tissues, it blocks the efficient metabolism of calcium and so makes the shell of an osprey's egg brittle, cracked by a touch of fingers. When a female settles down to incubate, she crushes her clutch beneath her.

Around the turn of the century, the ornithologist Alexander Wilson remarked that he saw osprey "thick about Rehoboth Bay," some twenty nests within a half-mile range. A concentrated colony flourished then at Cape Henlopen, with twenty-three nesting pairs, probably drawn by the dense schools of menhaden that crowded the waters of the lower bay. By 1972, when DDT was finally banned in the United States, populations of ospreys here and elsewhere along the northeast coast had plummeted to a small fraction of their former numbers. When Bill Frech came to Lewes in 1977, there were forty-six nesting pairs of osprey in all of Delaware. That year, observers across the bay at Cape May counted just over a thousand migrating osprey during the whole autumn season. Since the 1970s, the birds have somehow recovered their numbers. In October of 1989, nearly a thousand birds were spotted passing through Cape May on a single day. At last count, Delaware had seventy-five nests.

MOST OSPREYS ALONG THIS COAST make impressive annual migrations in orbit with the seasons, traveling south to the tropics in fall and north again in spring to breed. Young birds travel both ways alone. The migration route they follow is not learned, but acquired in the egg, carried in them by the accident of ancestry. A young osprey fledged in Lewes goes south to Peru or Venezuela to winter in the hot mists and vast swamps of the Amazon, and returns after a year or two to breed on the very same stretch of temperate shore where it fledged.

I know the gift of being able to find home is not allotted merely to these birds. Moose return annually to the same summer range. Bears transported more than fifty miles from their territory come back to it within days. Something in the cold brains of sea turtles guides them to their natal beaches after prodigious migrations of thousands of miles. Even limpets seem to know their way home, crawling back to a favorite scar or dimple on a rock at low tide, even if the face of the rock they cross has been hammered or chiseled into oblivion. Terns, swallows, gulls, and song sparrows, as well as shorebirds—piping plovers, ruddy turnstones, and sanderlings—all return to the same nesting ground in what is called *ortstreue*, or "place faithfulness." A strong attachment to birthplace makes good biological sense, of course. In a familiar landscape, animals have an easier time finding nesting sites and prey and avoiding predators. Biologist Ernst Mayr once remarked that birds have wings not so much for the purpose of getting away to a place but for the purpose of getting home.

Still, it seems astonishing that a young osprey, only a few months old, can take off over land and water and travel south three thousand miles; then, years later, head sure and direct, without guidance, back to the precise point of its infancy. Scientists believe that members of a pair stay together because they share a deep affinity for the same stretch of marsh or shore. Apparently ospreys carry an image of home in their heads that is sharp and well defined. How does a young bird register this place? What are its landmarks of sight and smell? Is it, as Lamarck said, that the environment creates the organ? Does our particular wash of blue and white bore those bright golden eyes and code the neurons that stream into those kinked wings? Do our mottled currents and patterns of marsh grass brand a bird, saying, Come toward this shore? There may be other sensual messages sent by the earth, undetected by us, but which a bird is innately prepared to receive. Although scientists suspect that some consciousness of the exact magnetic topology and field strength of a nesting area has something to do with it, no one really knows. "It's a black box sort of thing," one ornithologist told me. Somehow this stretch of shore works a kind of magic against all others to pull its progeny from the sky.

WHEN I WAS TWELVE, the school I went to sat on a hillside near a mature deciduous wood. At lunchtime, I often retreated to a small clearing some distance from the school to eat my sandwich and reflect on the morning's events. One day I sat on a log, peeling bark from a stick, and pondering the news that had struck our family a few weeks before: my father was leaving my mother. It was a warm, breezy day. Sunlight moving in and out of the clouds shattered the leafy surfaces with flecks of gold. I hadn't noticed trouble between my parents, engrossed as I was in my own awkward passing into adolescence. No shouting, no slamming doors. Suddenly this. The sunglasses my mother had been wearing for days couldn't conceal from me her wet face, her bafflement and sense of betrayal. I was at that age when I yearned above all else to be invisible, the way a Fowler's toad is invisible against the sand of the pine forest floor. The rift between my parents made me stand out and pick sides. It set me adrift, hunting for stable sanctuary in what had come to seem a shifting, unreliable world.

These woods were comforting and familiar. I knew their mossy hummocks and decaying stumps as well as any place I'd ever known. But this day I saw something new. Glancing up from the stick in my hand, I noticed a vibrating white dot about the size of a firefly in the trunk of an oak tree some distance from where I sat. It was more an absence than a presence, a tiny pulsating hole. I stared and stared.

The hole slowly grew into a crescent, then a large ragged horseshoe, a sizeable bite that should have split the tree in two. But the top half of the trunk just hung there like a stalactite. Still the hole grew, spreading in pulses until it swallowed nearby bushes and trees in white-hot light. It was as if my woods were being punched out or sucked up in a shiny boiling void. I couldn't shift my gaze from the growing hole, and a sense of horror stole over me. I got up and stumbled blindly out of the woods. By this time my hands were numb, dead weight at the ends of my arms, like dangling lumps of dough. Nausea roiled my insides; then a dot of hot pain shot through my temple and set the right side of my head throbbing.

This was my first experience with the aura of a classical migraine headache. The visual disturbance, the scintillating, zigzaggy chasm, is called a scotoma, meaning darkness or shadow. I rarely have such attacks anymore. I've learned to fend them off by lying down in darkness and focusing on that first tiny flash of white light, concentrating it until it shrinks into a pinpoint and pops out of existence. But I still think of that first aura not merely as a chaotic burst of firing among the thin wires of my brain but as a sudden, complete extinction of place.

Oddly enough, that pleat in my perception held a vision of the future. Several years later, when I returned to visit those woods, I found them gone. In their place was a thick cluster of row houses that clung like barnacles to the edge of the hill, and I was struck anew by a sense of disorientation and loss.

This sensation is not peculiar to humans. The loss of familiar surroundings, the destruction of refuge, is no doubt felt by animals, perhaps even more keenly than by our kind. I once saw something like this happen to a pair of osprey that for more than a decade had nested on a dilapidated pier behind the old fish factories. The pier was used in the 1950s and '60s to offload the giant nets of menhaden. When the factories closed, the pier fell into disuse; all that was left was a set of rotting pilings with a few cross timbers, disconnected from the land. One fall, developers bulldozed the fish factories to build condominiums and tore up the old pier. When the osprey returned that March, I watched them circle the empty water for hours in bewilderment. They hung around for days, perching on a nearby utility pole and watching the site, apparently recollecting a structure now made of air.

Stories are told of species that retain an image in their heads of places that have long disappeared. Monarchs migrating over Lake Superior fly south, then east, then south again, as if reading the echoes of a long-vanished glacier. Year after year, pilot whales on their autumn migrations strand themselves on the beaches of Cape Cod, as if unwilling to accept the presence of a twelve-thousand-year-old geological upstart that has parked itself in the middle of a migratory path they have followed for millions of years. American toads return to breed in ponds that have long since been paved over, drawn by some insubstantial vapor, some aura of home.

STUDIES OF HUMAN PREFERENCES for landscapes have found that our tribe tends to favor savannalike land—flat, grass-covered landscape studded with trees, where we had our origins and earliest home. Also promontories overlooking water. Some scientists even speculate that somewhere along the way we veered off the common primate course of evolution not just by swinging down from trees, but by going toward the sea. The seashore, with its abundance of edibles—fish, mollusks, turtle and bird eggs, digestible plants—and of shells, vines, kelp, and driftwood for tools, was the home of emergent humanity.

I like this idea that our earliest home landscapes are buried deep, embedded in our minds like an anchor at great depth, that we know in some dark, birdly way where we want to go.

Beauty may, indeed, lie in the genes of the beholder. Ospreys have been around for something like fifteen million years, long before we ever set foot on seashores. In our burgeoning minds, shore has never been separate from bird, so perhaps at some level, the two are joined in an inexplicable sweetness of union. Perhaps the osprey exists on a mental map of an earlier world passed down from our ancestors, and the bird in its landscape enters us like the parental. Perhaps it is also the other way around: Perhaps *he* contains *us* as part of his element, having seen us through the ages, through our infancy and the whole tumult of civilized man.

I wonder, too, if the residues of old ancestral landscapes don't rise up in our minds by the same deep grooves that make the scent of hay or sunlit ferns call up an episode from childhood, so that we act on buried instinct—like a dog at the hearth who turns slowly around and around on himself, tamping down a circle of imaginary grass— so that for the sake of marking her union in a meaningful way, a young bride puts up with salt stench and sand in her shoe.

Carol Muske

Coral Sea, 1945

for MY MOTHER

My mother is walking down a path
to the beach.
She has loosened her robe,
a blood-colored peignoir,
her belly freed
from the soft restraint of silk.
In a week I will be born.

Out on a reef
a small fleet waits for the end of the world.
My mother is not afraid.
She stares at the ships,
the lifting mask of coral,
and thinks: *the world is ending.*
The sea still orchid-colored before her
and to the south the ships in their same formation

but now the reef extends itself,
the sea thrusts up its odd red branches

each bearing a skeletal blossom.
I have no desire to be born.

In the coral sea
the parrots sing in their bamboo cages
the pearls string themselves in the mouths of the oysters
it snows inside the volcano
but no one believes these things.

And these things are not believable:
not the reef feeding itself
nor the ships moving suddenly, in formation.

Nor my body burning inside hers
in the coral sea
near the reef of her lungs

where I hung in the month of December.
In the year the war ended
the world opened,
ending for me
with each slow tremor
cold
invisible as snow
falling
inside the volcano.

Mark Jarman

Wave

Always offshore, or already broken, gone;
Foaming around the skin;
Its print embedded in the rigid sand;
Rising from almost nothing on the beach
To show its brood of gravel,
Then coming down hard, making its point felt.

Saying, "This time I mean it. This time I will
Not have to do it over;"
Repeating as if to perfect, as if,
Repeated, each were perfect; all forgotten,
One by one by one;
Every one, monster or beauty, going smash.

Wall after falling wall out to the sunset;
Or the ugly freak, capsizing
The fishing boat, reforming, riding on;
Still beautiful, lifting the frond of kelp,

Holding the silversides
Up to the eye, coming ashore in dreams.

Coming to light; invisible, appearing
To be the skeleton
Of water, or its muscle, or the look
Crossing its face; intelligence or instinct
Or neither; all we see
In substance moving toward us, all we wish for.

Already rising, lump in the throat, pulse
That taps the fingertip;
The word made flesh, gooseflesh; placid, the skin,
Remembering the sudden agitation,
Swelling again with pleasure;
All riders lifted easily as light.

Skin Cancer

Balmy overcast nights of late September;
Palms standing out in street light, house light;
Full moon penetrating the cloud-film
With an explosive halo, a ring almost half the sky;
Air like a towel draped over shoulders;
Lightness or gravity deferred like a moral question;
The incense in the house lit; the young people
Moving from the front door into the half-dark
And back, or up the stairs to glimpse the lovers' shoes
Outside the master bedroom; the youngest speculating;
The taste of beer, familiar as salt water;
Each window holding a sea view, charcoal
With shifting bars of white; the fog filling in
Like the haze of distance itself, pushing close, blurring.

As if the passage into life were through such houses,
Surrounded by some version of ocean weather,
Lit beads of fog or wind so stripped it burns the throat;
Mildew-spreading, spray-laden breezes and the beach sun
Making each grain of stucco cast a shadow;
An ideal landscape sheared of its nostalgia;
S. with his black hair, buck teeth, unsunned skin,
Joking and disappearing; F. doing exactly the same

But dying, a corkscrew motion through green water;
And C. not looking back from the car door,
Reappearing beside the East River, rich, owned, smiling at last.

Swains and nymphs. And news that came with the sea damp,
Of steady pipe-corrosions, black corners,
Moisture working through sand lots, through slab floors,
Slowly, with chemical, with molecular intricacy,
Then, bursting alive: the shrieked confessions
Of the wild parents; the cliff collapse; the kidnap;
The cache of photos; the letter; the weapon; the haunted dream;
The sudden close-up of the loved one's degradation.

Weather a part of it all, permeating and sanctifying,
Infiltrating and destroying; the sun disc,
Cool behind the veil of afternoon cloud,
With sun spots like flies crawling across it;
The slow empurpling of skin all summer;
The glorious learned flesh and the rich pallor
Of the untouched places in the first nakedness;
The working of the lesion now in late life,
Soon to be known by the body, even the one
Enduring the bareness of the inland plains,
The cold fronts out of Canada, a sickness
For home that feels no different from health.

Emma Aprile

Hawaii

the dirt here is blacker than space
richer than my dead grandfather

my father drives through the middle of Oahu
down a road cut into pineapple beds

I plunge my bare arms into the exposed dirt
touch roots of pineapple with my fingertips

shoots spring from my palms like stigmata
I am kneeling at the edge of asphalt

my father asks me to get back in the car
instead I slide farther into the pineapple bed

and I am blacker than space, richer than
the butter sauce we had last night on lobster

I am suffering in reverse
hands and feet explode into chloroplasts

green taste and chlorophyll roll across my tongue
shimmers of photosynthesis massage my scalp

the inside of my skin vibrates to a silent roar
I have become invisible

I am blacker than the void of space
fertile as lava swallowed by god

Mark Richard

Happiness of the Garden Variety

I felt really bad about what we ended up having to do to Vic's horse Buster today, not that, looking back, all this could have been helped, all this starting when Steve Willis and I were ripping the old roof off of where we live in the shanty by the canal on Vic's acres. Vic was up to Norfolk again, checking on a washing machine for his many-childed wife, Steve Willis and I left to rip off the roof and hammer in the new shingles. We were doing this in change for rent. Every month we do something in change for rent from Vic. Last month previous we strung three miles of pound net with bottom weights and cork toppers. What we change for rent usually comes to a lot more than what I'm sure the rent is for our four-room front porch shanty on the canal out back of Vic's, but Steve Willis and I like Vic and Vic lets us use his boat and truck for side business we do on new-moon nights.

Let me tell you something about what makes what we ended up doing to Vic's horse Buster all the worse. This is not to say about Vic less than Buster; me, I personally, and I know Steve Willis did too, hated Buster, Steve Willis having had to watch from far away Buster kill two of Vic's dogs. There'd be a stomp and a kick of dust and then a splash in the canal where it's a crab feast on old Tramp or Big Spot.

Then there was Buster's biting and kicking of us humans, Buster having bit me on my shoulder once coming up from behind while I was scraping barnacles from one of Vic's skiffs in change for rent and then he didn't even move when I came at him with a sharp-sided hoe. Steve Willis had Buster kick in the driver side of his car door after Buster had been into some weeds Vic had sprayed with the wrong powder. Buster kicked in the door so hard Steve Willis still has to crawl in from the other way. It was this eating that finally got Buster in the end, though not being able to read the right powder label is something about Vic which made him have us around.

This is what I mean, this about Vic and about what we did to his horse to make things all the worse: Vic could not read nor write, and this about Vic affected the way we all were with him. What I mean all, means Vic's wife and his children and Buster and his dogs and all the acres we all lived on down by the canal, and everything on all the acres, and everything on all those acres painted aquamarine blue, because one thing about Vic, and I say this to show how Steve Willis and I made this all the worse, was that Vic not reading or writing seemed to make him not to think about things like they had names that he had to remember by way of thinking that needed spelling, but instead Vic seemed to think about things in groups, like here is a group of things that are my humans, here is a group of things that are my animals, here is a group of things I got for free, here is a group of things I got off good deal-making, and here is a group of things I should keep a long time because I got them from some people who had kept them a long time, and maybe because of a couple of these reasons put together, Vic had another group of things painted aquamarine blue because he had gotten a good deal on two fifty-five-gallon barrels of aquamarine paint, and everything—even Vic's humans and animals who could not help but rub against or sit in somewhere because it was everywhere wet—everything was touched the color of aquamarine, though all of us calling it *ackerine,* because even spelling it out and sounding it out to Vic it still came out of his mouth that way, ackerine, keeping in mind here is a man who can't read nor write, and Steve Willis and I always saying it ackerine like Vic said it, for fun, because it also always seemed like somehow we were always holding a brush of it somewhere putting it on something in change for rent.

So what made what we did to Buster worse were some ways in Vic's thinking which were brought on by him not reading nor writing. Just because somebody had kept Buster a long time to Vic made it seem Buster was very valuable, and even though the horse did come with some history tied to it, the real reason the people had Buster for so long was because they were old and could not seem to kill the horse by just shooting it with bird shot over and over even though they tried again and again, them just making Buster meaner and easier for Vic to buy when the two old people saw him in church and asked did he want a good deal on a historical horse. The history Buster had was he was the last of the horses they used at Wicomico Light Station to run rescue boats into the surf. To Steve Willis and I when we heard it said So what? but to Vic this was some history he could understand and appreciate, being an old sailor himself and it being some facts that did not have to be gotten from a history book that he could not read from in the first place.

What I came to find out later on was the heart tug Vic felt about this old horse that had to do with when Vic grew up, Vic's father having boarded a team of surf horses in a part of the house Vic slept in when he was a boy because all the children from Vic's parents spilled out of the two-room clapboard laid low in the dunes, not a far situation from Vic's own children who as long as Steve Willis and I have lived here I don't think I have seen all of yet because they keep spilling out of the house barefoot all year around and maybe it's because there are so many of them that Vic can't seem to remember all their names right rather than the fact he can't place in his mind what they are called because Vic cannot read nor write.

Anyway, the point I'm leading to about the heart tug is that where Vic spent his life as a child was sleeping with two other brothers in a hayloft over a team of old surf horses, and a hayloft mostly empty at that, not even because there was no hay to be had on an island of sand but because the team always grazed on the wild sea oats in the dunes, and this is what makes what we did the worse, this tug on Vic's heart to his younger days that Buster had, me hearing Vic tell it all to Buster one day when Vic didn't know I did, the feeling Vic remembered best of laying snug with his brothers, all of them laid all over each other to keep warm during the winter northeasters that shook the two-room clapboard and the tacked-on horse stalls where they slept, remembering them in the early mornings keeping warm wishing for breakfast while down below the horses would be stirring to go out, making droppings and the smell coming up to the warm, all-over-each-other brothers, the warm smell of wild sea oats passed through the two solid horses breathing sea fog breath.

So that was the heart tug Buster had and I don't mean to make Vic out strange owing to him liking the smell of an old horse passing gas, I think if you think about it there's really nothing there that doesn't fit with a man not thinking thoughts he has to read nor write, but fits well with a man who thinks of things as being good when they are human or animal especially if they came about by getting them free or from off a good deal.

I guess that is the main reason about Vic besides using his boat and truck on new-moon nights that Steve Willis and I stuck around, us in a couple of groups in Vic's mind mainly getting a good deal off of, us stringing nets, ripping roofs, and painting everything not breathing what we called ackerine, and that is also the main reason what we ended up doing ended up all the worse.

So like I said, this all started when Steve Willis and I were ripping the old roof off our four-room front porch shanty by the canal in change for rent. Vic had gone to Norfolk because he had heard of a good deal some people from church told him about to do with washing machines, and Vic, having stood in water barefoot while plugging his old washer in and getting thrown against a wall by the shock, naturally to his mind thought it was broken and in need of replacing. Vic had left in the morning coming in to get Steve Willis and I up around dawn to finish the roof and said only one other simple thing, the real easy thing, to please keep Buster out of the garden no matter what we did. Then Vic was off through the gate in his good-deal truck he had painted ackerine blue one night after supper the week before.

It was July hot, and before we started Steve Willis and I just walked around our shanty roof, just looking, because the island we live on is flat with just scrub pine and wandering dunes and from the single story up you can see Wicomico Light, the inlet bridge, and the big dunes where the ocean breaks beyond. It was a good morning knowing Vic's wife would come soon out bringing us some sticks of fried fish wrapped in brown paper, her knowing for breakfast we usually had a cigarette and a Dr. Pepper. For a long time Steve Willis and I had not made any new-moon runs to Stumpy Point to make us watch the one lane down to Vic's acres for cars we wouldn't like the looks of and I could look at Steve Willis and Steve Willis could look at me and we could feel good to be one of Vic's humans in a house on all of Vic's acres.

About midway through the morning after their chores about a half a dozen of Vic's kids came spilling barefoot out of Vic's ackerine blue house to ride the ackerine bicycles and tricycles and to play on the good-deal ackerine swing set and jungle gym. The older Vic's kids got to play fishing boat and battleship down on the canal dock as long as one of them stayed lookout to keep a count of heads and to watch for snakes.

From over my shoulder I was watching what Buster was up to. He stood looking up at me in the middle of the midday morning hot yard not seeking shade like even a common ass would but just standing in the yard near where the incline made of good-deal railway ties came out of the canal and led on up to the boat shed. Buster stood not even slapping his tail at the blackflies that were starting to work on Steve Willis and I up on the roof ripping shingles, but standing so still as if knowing not to attract one bit of attention to himself on his way to he and I knew where. I would rip a row of shingles and then look over my shoulder and Buster would be standing perfectly still not even slapping his tail at the blackflies or even showing signs of breath in and out of his big almost-to-the-ground-slouching belly. Just standing as if he was a big kid's toy some big kid was moving around in the yard when I wasn't looking, all the time moving closer by two or three feet at a time to the garden.

So I would rip a row and look, rip a row and look, never seeing him move even by an inch, and I saw Steve Willis was not even bothered by looking to keep an eye on Buster out of the garden even though Vic had told us both to do it, and the reason was a simple one for Steve Willis not to care, and boiled down, this is it: the evening Vic went over to make the good deal off the old people who had Buster for so long he rode Buster home and when he showed up at the gate needing one of us, me or Steve Willis to come down off the porch of our shanty to open the gate, it was me who came down to let Vic and Buster in the yard. That is the reason for Steve Willis not caring about Buster, not one thing more. Steve Willis stayed on the porch with his feet up on the railing watching Vic ride Buster by and me close the gate, and ever since, anything Vic tells us to do or about or with Buster, it is me who does it or me who listens even though Vic is telling us both, it is me and not Steve Willis, all from me getting down to open the gate that one time. That is why today Steve Willis was just ripping rows and not looking at Buster sneak, and I tell you, this forward thinking in Steve Willis when we make our new-moon runs, I like it then, but around the chores in Vic's back acres it can become tiresome and make you job-shy yourself.

Just about lunch time, just about the time for the little Vic's children to come into their house to get cold pieces of fried fish and Kool-Aid for lunch, the big Vic's children down by the dock all shouted Snake! and ran about fetching nets, poles, and paddles. This was a good time for Steve Willis and I to break so Steve Willis and I broke for a cigarette to watch what would all Vic's kids be telling around the table that night all supper long. Vic's big kids ran up and back the dock trying to catch the snake with their poles and paddles, and the poor snake swam from side to side in the boat slip with his escape cut off by one of Vic's big kids poling around in a washtub trailing a minnow seine. One of Vic's big girl kids caught the tired-out snake on the surface and dipped him out with a canoe paddle and one of Vic's big boys grabbed it up and snapped it like a bullwhip, popping its neck so it went limp. Vic's dogs that Buster hadn't yet kicked into the canal barked and jumped up on the boys playing keep-away with the snake until the boys took it up to the outside sink where we clean fish to skin it out and dry what the dogs didn't eat in the sun.

As they all paraded up to the house I came to notice the yard seemed even emptier than it should have been with Vic's kids and dogs all gone up to the big house, then I realized what piece was missing when between the wooden staked-out rows of peabeans I saw a patch of sparrow-shot ragged horsehair and a big horse behind showing out by the tomatoes. I shouted a couple of times and spun a shingle towards where Buster was at work munching cabbage and cucumbers but the shingle just skipped off his big horse behind and splashed into the canal.

By the time I got down from the roof leaving Steve Willis up there ripping shingles, Steve Willis not being the one to open the gate that first time Buster came to Vic's acres, Buster had eaten half the young cabbage heads we had. I knew better than to come up from behind a horse who can kick a full-grown collie thirty yards so I picked up the canoe paddle the big Vic's girl had used to fling up the snake on the dock with and went through the corn to cut Buster off at the cabbage.

But head to head, me shouting and making up and down wild slicing actions with the canoe paddle, Buster had no focus on me. Instead he was stopped in mid-chew. Then the sides of his almost-to-the-ground-slouched belly heaved out, then in, and then more out, moving so much more out that patches of horsehair popped and dropped off and I took a half step backward fearing for an explosion. I called for Steve Willis to come down, to hurry up, but all Steve Willis said was what did I want, and I said I think Buster is sick from whatever Vic had sprayed on the cabbage, probably not getting anybody to read the label of what it was to begin with, and then

Buster side-stepped like he was drunk through two rows of stake-strung peabeans, and then he pitched forward to where I was backing up holding the canoe paddle, of little good, I was thinking, against an exploding horse, and then Buster, I swear before God, Buster erupt-belched and blew out broken wind loudly at the other end at the exact same time as his knees shook out from under him and he went down among the tallest tomatoes in Vic's garden wiping out the uneaten cabbage and some cucumber pickles too.

By this time Steve Willis had come down off the roof to look at the tragedy we were having in Vic's garden. It was hard to count the amount of summer suppers Buster had ruint and smushed. Steve Willis called Buster a son of a bitch for wiping out the tomatoes, Steve Willis' favorite sandwich being tomato with heavy pepper and extra mayonnaise.

Steve Willis asked me did I hit Buster in the head or what with the canoe paddle but I promised I hadn't given him a lick at all with it, though we were both looking at how hard I was holding on to the handle. Steve Willis pushed in on Buster's big blowing-up belly with his toe and air started to hiss out of Buster's mouth like a nail-struck tire, and the fear of explosion having not completely passed, we both stepped back. You could tell the little hiss was coming out near where Buster's big black and pink tongue stuck pretty far out of his mouth laying in the dirt between where the tomatoes were smushed and the cabbage used to be.

Steve Willis said This is not good.

Usually when Steve Willis and I have a problem in our on-the-side new-moon business, we say we have to do some Big Thinking, and we are always seeming to be doing Big Thinking in all our business, but since this was a Buster problem and since Steve Willis didn't come down off the porch that first time to open the gate, it was coming clear to me I would have to be the Big Thinker on this one. I stepped away to think really big about the tragedy, figuring from where the garden is situated around the boat shed by our shanty on the canal you can't see it from the big house. I figured I had a fair while to figure where to go with Buster after I got him out of the garden, hoping to find a hole enough nearby for such a big animal and do it all while Vic's little children slept out of the afternoon sun and while Vic's big children went to afternoon Bible study.

In the first part of thinking big I went up to the garage to get the good-deal riding lawn mower to yank Buster out until I remembered it had a broken clutch, and when I came back Steve Willis was holding back a laugh to himself, and I will say about Steve Willis, he is not one to laugh right in your face. He was holding back a laugh, holding the rope I'd given him to put around Buster to yank him out. Steve Willis asked me what kind of knot would I suggest he tie a dead horse to a broken riding lawn mower with.

I could see how far I could get Steve Willis to help with the Buster tragedy so I took the line out of his hand and put a timber hitch around one of Buster's hind legs saying out loud A timber hitch seems to work pretty well thanks a whole hell of a lot. I paid the line out from the garden and started to get that sinking feeling of a jam panic, a jam closing in needing Very Big Thinking, with not the July hot sun in the yard baking waves of heat making me feel any better at all. You get that sinking jam panic feeling, and I got it so bad that while I was paying out the line across the yard, and even though I knew I could not ever possibly do it, I stopped and held hard to the line and gave it a good solid pull the hardest I could to yank Buster out, straining, pulling, even when I saw when it was hopeless, and

MARK RICHARD | 81

even with the jam panic worse, I had to let go of the line, and all the difference I had made was that now there was air hissing out from where blackflies were moving around and settling back beneath Buster's big stringy tail.

This was even better than before to Steve Willis who stepped behind what tall tomatoes were left so he wouldn't have to laugh at me to my face. I picked up a shingle I'd flung at Buster from the roof and spun it towards Steve Willis but it sliced to the right and shattered our side kitchen window and Steve Willis had to go behind the boat shed to laugh not in my face this time after you couldn't hear glass falling in the shanty anymore.

I gathered up the line bunched at my feet and trailed it over to the boat shed down to the dock. Vic's big Harker Island rig, our new-moon boat with the Chrysler inboard was gassed up with the key rusted in the ignition. I cleated the line that ran across the yard from Buster's hind leg onto the stanchion on the stern and shouted over to Steve Willis in the garden to at least help me throw off the lines.

I felt for an instant better starting up the big deep-throated engine so that the floorboards buzzed my feet, feeling the feeling I get that starts to set in running the rig over to the hidden dock on the south bay shore on new-moon nights, the feeling of the chance of sudden money and the possibility of anything, even danger and death, and feeling now in a July hot sun the feeling of Big Thinking a way out of a bad tragedy. With the engine running it was now possible in my mind that we wouldn't lose our place of life in Vic's acres over something like letting a big horse die.

I was feeling better as Steve Willis threw off the stern line and I choked the wraps on the stanchion leading to where I could just see two big-legged hooves hung up in the tomatoes where I could snatch

Buster out and decide what to do then, but the sound of the big engine turning over brought out the dogs from underneath the big house, them being used to going out with Vic in the mornings to check five miles of pound net, and then some of the older kids not yet set off for Bible study started to spill out of the house to see what Steve Willis and I were up to this time with their daddy's boat, and if I looked harder at the house, which I did, I could see the little Vic's children in the windows with diapers and old Vic's t-shirts on wanting to follow the big kids out, but not coming, them having to sleep in away from the July hot sun.

Vic's dogs got down to us first, and even old Lizzie's tan and gray snout, a snout she lets babies pull without snapping, and a snout which would, when you were bent over fooling with getting the lawn hose turned on, come up and give you a friendly goose in your rear end, even old Lizzie's tan and gray snout snarled back to show ripping wolflike teeth when she saw that old bastard of a horse Buster was down, and then she and all of Vic's other dogs were on the carcass and there was no keeping them away.

Now I had the problem of everybody in Vic's acres coming down to see what I had let happen to Buster, topped off by the dogs having their day going after Buster's body biting his hind legs and ripping away at the ears and the privates. The sight of the dogs on Buster was no less than the sounds they made, blood wild, and here came the rest of the kids to see all this, this even being better than chasing the watersnake around and out of the canal for a supper-table story.

I had to Big Think quick so I pulled Steve Willis by his belt into the boat, us starting over at that point about me and him and anything to do with Buster, forgetting that first time him not getting down to open the gate. I pushed forward on the throttle but did it swinging the bow off where I knew the sand bar was, still being in the right mind to know not to double up a dead horse tragedy with bad boatsmanship. When I rounded the dock and the line leading to where the pack of wild-acting animals were in the tomatoes with the horse carcass snugged tight, our bow rose and our stern squared, and I really gave the big old lovey Chrysler the gas and, looking over my shoulder, I saw Buster slide from the garden with still the dogs around, this time giving chase to the dragging legs, because in their simple minds they were probably thinking the only way to stop something with legs is to bite its feet whether that something is standing on them or not.

I knew that I was not just pulling Buster out of the garden now but that we had him sort of in tow, so that as we turned onto the canal proper and Buster skidded across the bulkhead and onto the dock that I knew wouldn't take his weight, I really had to pour the engine on, and I was right, Buster's big body humped the bulkhead over and came down splintering the dock we had just been tied to, but for an instant even over the dogs barking and the children yelling and the deep-throated throttle of the engine giving me any of anything making me feel better about all of this, just for an instant I heard Buster's hooves hit and clotter across the good-deal planking of the dock before bringing it down, and in that second of hearing horse's hooves on plank I had to turn back quick and look, because it passed over me that maybe I would see Buster galloping behind us giving chase to me and Steve Willis out of Vic's garden instead of us dragging his big dead body out to sea in tow.

We still had plenty of canal to cover before we broke out into open ocean. The dogs raced along beside us on the bank of the canal as far as they could but it was a game to them now, their wolf-like leaps mellowed out into tongue-flapping lopes. A couple of neighbors on down the canal came out to watch and the wake and spray from Buster cutting along ass backwards threw water into their yards. One of Vic's cousins, Malcolm, was working in a boat and seeing us coming he held up a pair of waterskis pointing to Buster laughing as we passed, but I could see open ocean so I throttled down and leaned hard forward to balance against the rising bow. I was glad I had enough forward thinking of my own to pull Steve Willis into the boat starting us over about Buster because I could look at him in the stern watching the big horse carcass we had in tow by a stiffed up leg, and looking at Steve Willis I could see it was sinking in on him that when Vic came home from Norfolk and threw me out of the back acres by the canal it would be Steve Willis himself being thrown out too.

I burned up about three hours of fuel looking for the right place to cut Buster loose. One problem we had was one time we stopped to idle the engine and pull up a floorboard so I could check the oil and while we set to drifting Steve Willis noticed that Buster floated. You could tell how the body was like a barrel just below the surface that it was the air or the gas or whatever was in Buster's big belly keeping him afloat. When I got up from checking the oil I threw to where Steve Willis was standing in the stern a marlin spike and he looked down at the spike and then he looked up to me like he was saying Oh no I won't punch a hole, and I looked back at him wiping the oil off my hands, looking back like Oh yes you will punch a hole, and when it came time for me to cut Buster loose out near the number-nine sea buoy and it came time for Steve Willis to punch a hole, I did and he did and it was done.

So here we are really feeling bad about what we finally ended up doing to Vic's horse Buster, us drinking about it in the First Flight Lounge after we called Vic's wife at home and she said Un huh and

Nunt uh to the sideways questions we asked her about Vic being home yet, trying to feel out how bad was the tragedy, and her hanging up not saying goodbye, and us wondering did she always do that and then us realizing we'd never talked to her on the telephone before.

After we tied up Vic's rig in the ditch behind the First Flight Lounge we started to wonder if shouldn't we have let Vic had his say about what to do with his finally dead horse, so therein started us having the lack of forward thinking and of Big Thinking, and instead we were left to second guessing and after we had left the rig with its better-feeling hum and came in to drink, with the drink buzzes coming on ourselves, we started to feel naked in our thinking, especially when a neighbor of Vic's came in and shook his head when he saw us and then walked back out.

So what Steve Willis and I have done is to get down off the wall the tide chart and figure out where the most likely place for Buster to wash in is. We'll head out over there when the tide turns and wait for Buster to come in on the surf and then drag him up to take him home in a truck we'll somehow Big Think our way to fetch by morning. The tide tonight turns at about two thirty, just about when the lounge closes, too, so that is when we think we will make our move to the beach in front of the Holiday Inn, which is where we expect Buster back.

So Steve Willis and I sit in the First Flight Lounge not having the energy to begin to think about where we are to live after having to get ready to be kicked out of Vic's acres, much less having the energy to Big Think about pulling a sea-bloated horse out of the surf at two thirty in the morning. Here we are sitting not having the energy to Big Think about all of this when Vic walks in barefooted and says Gintermen, ginterman, another one of the ways he says things because he can't read nor write and doesn't know how things are spelled to speak them correct.

There is a nervous way people who don't drink, say, preachers, act in bars but that is not Vic. Vic sits at our table open-armed and stares at all the faces in the place, square in the eye, including our own we turn down. He sits at the table that is for drinking like it could be a table for anything else. Vic says he saw his rig tied up in the ditch behind the lounge on his way home from Norfolk, would we want a ride home and come get it in the morning.

Steve Willis and I settle up and stand to go out with Vic who says he's excited about the good deal he's come back with. Looking at Steve Willis I still see it's to me to start telling Vic about us having to wait for his favorite animal in his animal group to wash up down the beach, all at our hands.

Out in back of Vic's truck Vic runs his hands over six coin washing machines, something he does to all his new good-deal things to make them really his own. Vic says he got them from a business that was closing down, won't his wife be happy. Vic says our next change for rent will be to rewire the machines so they can run without putting in the quarters, what did we think. I start to tell Vic about Buster and the tragedy in the garden. I can't see Vic in the dark when they turn off the front lights to the First Flight Lounge but I can hear him say Un huh, un huh as I talk.

When I finish the part with Steve Willis and I waiting for the tide to turn Vic says Come on boys, we ought to get on home oughten we. All three of us sit up front of the truck riding across the causeway bridges home. All Vic says for a while is Well, my horse, my old horse, not finishing the rest, if there is anything to finish, and I get the feeling Vic is rearranging groups in his mind like his animal group things and his human group things and his good-deal-off-people things, and maybe making a new group of really awful people things with just me and Steve Willis in it.

But then Vic starts talking about how in change for rent Steve Willis and I are also going to build a laundry platform with a cement foundation and a pine rafter shedding, and Vic starts to talk like, even after taking rearrangement of all his things in all his groups, everything still comes up okay. Vic says oughten we lay the foundation around near the downside of the shanty where Steve Willis and I live so the soap water can drain into the canal, and after we figure how to put the sidings and braces up, oughten we put a couple of coats of paint on it to keep the weather out, maybe in change for some rent, and what color would us boys say would look good, and Steve Willis and I both sit forward and yell Ackerine! at the same time, us all laughing, and me feeling, crossing the last causeway bridge home, I'm happy heading there as a human in Vic's acres again.

Yusef Komunyakaa

Newport Beach, 1979

To them I'm just a crazy nigger
out watching the ocean
drag in silvery nets of sunfish,
dancing against God's spine—
if He's earth, if He's a hunk of celestial bone,
if He's real as Superman
holding up the San Andreas Fault.

Now look, Miss Baby Blue Bikini,
don't get me wrong.
I'm not the Redlight Bandit,
not Mack the Knife, or Legs Diamond
risen from the dead
in a speak-easy of magenta sunsets perpetually
overshadowing nervous breakdowns.

I'm just here where first-degree eyes
look at me like loaded dice,
as each day hangs open

in hurting light like my sex
cut away & tied to stalks
of lilies, with nothing else
left to do for fun.

Boat People

After midnight they load up.
A hundred shadows move about blindly.
Something close to sleep
hides low voices drifting
toward a red horizon. Tonight's
a black string, the moon's pull—
this boat's headed somewhere.
Lucky to have gotten past
searchlights low-crawling the sea,
like a woman shaking water
from her long dark hair.

Twelve times in three days
they've been lucky,
clinging to each other in gray mist.
Now Thai fishermen gaze out across
the sea as it changes color,
hands shading their eyes
the way sailors do,
minds on robbery & rape.
Sunlight burns blood-orange.

Storm warnings crackle on a radio.
The Thai fishermen turn away.
Not enough water for the trip.
The boat people cling to each other,
faces like yellow sea grapes,
wounded by doubt & salt.
Dusk hangs over the water.
Seasick, they daydream Jade Mountain
a whole world away, half-drunk
on what they hunger to become.

Gray Jacobik

Sandwoman

The woman lay firm in the damp berm of the beach—
she flowed into it and was contiguous with it,
was, in fact, formed of it. The sky chinked through
its hours, its gradations of sky-hues, the azures,
ceruleans, deeper blues, and the golds and roses
of evening. Sky was all she could see, all she
opened her legs to, all her breasts and belly strove
to touch. The sum of her changes were color
and cloud—until the lips of the sea reached her—
those lascivious lips bruised by the moon.
Seafoam threw its lace shawl over her shoulders
and fans of lace shrouded her face. Slowly, slowly,
in licks, and then sometimes in spills, the sea
overcame her, her wavy hair running down the beach,
right breast and then left breast crumbling like turrets.
Waves gathered back the seaweed of her pubis,
then licked at her sex until she dissolved the way,
so tasted, all women dissolve. She had given her
heart to the blinding smack of noonday light

and to the soft coruscations of the lamb-back clouds
that traversed her body through the late afternoon,
until she was only a shadow by night. The one who
shaped her with hands knew that love falls through
the body like sand, and the whole of the erotic sculpts
our limbs and faces, teases wide the splay of our legs.

Heat Wave

Integers of seethe, digits of sizzle;
the week's exceptional heat-index
compounds itself, refuses compromise.

We wear shorts or underwear or nothing.
A light dust of snowy talc. The drone
of fans becomes its own encasement.

Complaints unfold their premises,
nerves are threadbare. Fabrications
need a cool breeze to fly upon, so no

lies, no stories. Stubborn truth stands
steadfast and unadorned. It is too hot
for embellishments. Even the arrogant

grow shy in this weather. Bodies lose
their separate-from-space edges, and
our lives, like our roads, blur into

mirages. Glare-thick daylight dissolves
against a too-white sky: a fade into
a fade into a fade. Desires dissipate.

Even the hills have sterner silences.
A noose around the pond, the duckweed's
stranglehold tightens. Algae spread like

cholera. No fly-casting fishermen crack
whips over the river. And the handyman laid
his tools down on the porch and wandered off,

drunk perhaps, or stupefied with heat.

Sallie Bingham
Off-Season

Never, no matter who warned her, would Missy have believed what happened next: Daddy, calling from Miami, "Get on home, there's trouble," when she wouldn't ever go back to that house full of three marriages' worth of children (Daddy always won custody and maintenance, the two went together); all her three mamas—as they called themselves (her real one was dead), but they never phoned, thinking Good Riddance; any of her half-this and half-that—she had enough half-relatives to decorate a tree; or that creep Hart, her boyfriend he liked to call himself, who never even offered to walk her through those screaming meemies outside the clinic.

Her family had written her off after her second DUI and were pleased as punch she'd moved in with the High Roller (as they called him; she just called him Jimmy) where there was plenty to keep a blonde twenty-year-old girl busy, especially one with old-fashioned long hair and high arches like a dancer. The only problem in Key West was finding a place to live.

The person who did call her finally was some creep from an outfit called Findem Inc. It seemed Jimmy's wife up in Chicago (just as good as divorced) had all of a sudden gotten antsy about who was in the house on Simonton, where Missy had just gotten herself settled, with her shell collection on the bar and her beer mug collection on the windowsill over the kitchen sink.

She told the Findem guy who was in the house that it was no business of Jimmy's ex. The fool had deeded the house over lock, stock, and barrel to her handsome then-husband, and so what if she had paid? There are no fools like old fools, Missy reminded the Findem guy, and he agreed.

Then he told her the real shocker: According to some ancient Florida law, property belongs to both spouses no matter whose name is on the deed. She'd just about died.

"She wants to make trouble," Jimmy said when he called, with the little-boy catch in his voice that made Missy want to reach out and ruffle his curls. She'd caught sight of a bottle in the shower that made her suspicious he dyed them, but so what? It was the heart that mattered, and Jimmy had a lot of heart, which was why he kept taking grief from his soon-to-be ex. He even claimed he still loved her, which would have irked Missy if she'd believed it.

"She claims you've defiled our bed," Jimmy said.

Missy blinked. "To hell with her, I take a bath every night."

Jimmy sighed. She could feel the sound coming down the telephone line like a warm little cloud.

"Helen's just irrational," he said.

"Eaten up by the green-eyed monster. If she sets such store by this bed, why isn't she in it?"

"Well, honey, you're in it, for one thing," Jimmy said.

Missy dragged on her cigarette, and a thin stream of smoke spiraled up into the white lace stuff that hung from the top of the bed. She propped one foot on her knee and noticed the red polish on her right big toe was scuffed from putting on her sandal too soon. She sighed, sending Jimmy a little warm puff all his own.

"You're not listening, sweetheart," Jimmy said.

"You haven't said much."

"Well then, get ready: She's going down to Key West Saturday."

Missy tried to remember what day it was. "Oh shit," she said.

"I hate to say this, but I'm afraid you're going to have to move out for a day or two," Jimmy said.

Missy considered her options. She was not going back to the trailer she'd been sharing with Lee Ann, a waitress from Pensacola—that was definitely not part of her plan. Lee Ann was mean; Missy believed all girls with men's names had a mean streak.

Going down the list, she thought about Oswald-the-Mechanic (as she called him, after the name on his panel truck), but he'd left for a week's fishing in the upper Keys and his mother had his room locked up tight; even nailed down the window because of that tree they used to climb. And the motels, even off-season, were too expensive or closed—Jimmy would probably object to paying; he didn't like to throw around money, which was the first sign she'd had that he wasn't quite what he claimed.

Not that she cared: She loved him no matter what, which was the reason she was biting her tongue when she wanted to give him hell.

"I am not going back to that park bench. Nine nights sleeping outdoors is enough."

She heard him catch his breath. "I'd never let you do that."

The catch did it; she knew she was in safe water.

"I'm not moving," she said.

Next day Missy saw a big brown suitcase sitting on the front step, half an hour after the last puddle jumper came in from Miami.

She was sitting out of the rain on the upstairs porch, looking at a book she'd bought at the Piggly-Wiggly; it took only a little forward motion of her head to see the big brown suitcase and then the ex herself, paying off old Paul. She must have given him a big tip from the way he was bowing and scraping. Then the ex started toward the front steps and Missy stood up.

She saw the gray hair pinned on the back of the head and the leather handbag on the shoulder strap and the pricey silk suit, all of which she'd seen before on homeowners coming in for their vacations. Never this time of year, though, never off-season.

She went downstairs, knowing the lady was watching her through the glass front door—bare feet, cutoffs, skinny T-shirt, and all.

"Hello," the lady said when Missy opened the door.

"I'm not expecting company," Missy said, keeping her hand on the knob.

The lady had a sharp set to her lips that reminded Missy of her seventh-grade English teacher, but she was misty-looking, too. "We need to talk," she said.

Missy stretched her hands over her head and yawned—a fake. "Why do you want to come in here?"

"Because this is my house," the lady said, fumbling in her handbag.

"That's not what Jimmy told me."

"Nobody," the lady said, "calls him Jimmy."

"Well, I do." She let go of the doorknob, and the lady stepped in.

"I'm Helen Whitehouse," she said, holding out her hand.

Missy took it between her finger and thumb. She smelled Helen's perfume, a thin clear lavender. Her hand felt solid, had weight. She looked at Helen's long arms and legs, the feet planted in flat leather sandals. Then she glanced at the pale sharp face; her blue eyes had that shine.

"Hello," Missy said.

The afternoon went quickly to the tune of heavy rain and ceiling fans stroking the air. At the end of the first hour, Missy put a few things in her day pack and moved to the back bedroom; when she heard Helen snapping sheets off the four-poster bed, she went to help her. They both liked tight-drawn sheets. Missy complimented Helen on her color choice: shell-pink. The ones waiting to be washed were lavender.

An hour later they were sitting under the awning that sheltered the bar at Miriam's, looking out over the gray water. Helen listened while Missy told about her daddy and her three mamas and the tribe of half-this and half-that and the screamers at the clinic. That last got Helen; she put her hand to her mouth. "I have a daughter your age," she said. "To think she might have to go through an ordeal like that."

"Probably already has," Missy said.

"Oh, I'm sure she would have told me."

"I thank you for not making me leave," Missy said, switching the subject. She thought it was safe to say that now, though there'd been no invitation.

Helen Whitehouse stared. Then she sighed. "When I go Monday, you will have to leave."

Missy nodded. She knew two days could turn up all kinds of possibilities: Jimmy might come back or Hart might resurface, calling her from a pay phone to say he was sorry.

"You've had quite a life," Helen said. "My daughter hasn't seen much yet."

"What's her name?"

"Helen," Helen said proudly.

Missy could just see her, blonde hair cut yesterday and a younger version of her mother's sharp-edged face. She decided to try some sugar. "Any girl that's got Jimmy for a dad—"

"Jimmy's not her father," Helen said. "He's my second husband." She made him sound like a medal, maybe not first place but surely reserve champion. "Seven years," Helen said. "That's not so bad. Of course we have our ups and downs."

Missy thought how her up was Helen's down, and vice versa.

Then Angie came by with a tray of clean glasses. She did a double take when she saw Missy perched on the bar stool. "Look what the cat drug in! Pardon me," she said to Helen.

"Are you two friends?" Helen asked.

"We used to work together," Missy said.

"Till Missy got too big for her britches," Angie said, lining the glasses up on the shelf behind the bar.

"How was that?" Helen asked.

"We're here to enjoy ourselves," Missy said, but Angie never would take a hint.

"She has a mouth on her," Angie told Helen.

"So that's how you ended up on the park bench." Helen reached over to touch the back of Missy's small tanned hand.

Later, back at the house, they defrosted some crabmeat in the microwave and ate it with butter. It was soggy, but it was a Key West specialty and Missy was glad she'd suggested it. Then they sat on the deck and drank coffee and Kahlúa and watched the moon sail from cloud to cloud. Helen fixed their second round in little gold-edged cups she'd hidden at the back of a cabinet; from that, Missy knew Helen had guessed Jimmy was up to something—women only hide things when they know what's going on.

Later the phone rang in the living room, but neither of them answered it. The wind stirred the frangipani by the deck, and it dropped its long white flowers on the surface of the pool. Helen took Missy's hand again and read her life-line: "You'll live to be a hundred."

"I don't think I want to," Missy said.

"Oh, but you must."

Later Missy listened to the answering machine, heard Jimmy's voice, and erased it.

Still later Helen asked Missy what Jimmy was "like—you know," embarrassed but smiling. Missy said, "He moans a lot." They were sitting on the four-poster bed with drinks in their hands.

"He used to do that with me," Helen said.

"It wears off."

"Does he have any, you know, problems?"

"He's a little bit soon, sometimes."

"He's always had trouble with that," Helen said.

"I don't mean it's anything real bad—"

"No, of course not—he can't help it. But don't you find it means..." She let her pretty quicksilver voice trail off.

"I have a vibrator," Missy said. Its brown cord was hanging out from under the bed.

"I ordered one of those once from a catalog, but when it came I threw it in the trash."

"Why'd you do that?"

"It seemed a little...indecent. And I thought Jimmy might be hurt."

"I just tell him I'm taking care of myself."

"And he accepts that?"

Missy nodded. "It takes the monkey off his back."

Before bedtime, Helen filled the big marble bathtub with hot water and pink oil and invited Missy to step in. When she stood in the tub, Missy saw herself reflected four times over in the mirrors that lined the walls.

She sat down in the hot foamy water, and Helen began to scrub her back with the long-handled brush. "You have a lovely tan," Helen said.

"I work on it every day there's sun," Missy told her.

Around midnight Helen tucked her in bed, kissed her ear, and turned out the light. "Sleep tight," she said as she went out, but Missy, snuggling deep into the pure-down pillows, was already asleep.

IT TURNED OUT Helen had had a hard life, in a way. She'd married some slob when she was nineteen, and of course he drank. "Who doesn't?" Missy asked. As soon as Helen had unloaded him, along came Jimmy who looked promising, with that shy way of staring off into the distance as though he was looking for his particular star. Now the same thing was starting all over again, Helen said: the drinking—she'd found bottles hidden all over the house.

It was the next morning when they talked about Jimmy's drinking; they were down on their hands and knees, scrubbing the kitchen floor. Missy hated housework, but Helen insisted it would be therapeutic and a bond.

"Does he get drunk with you?" Helen asked, but Missy couldn't really say. Jimmy always had a glass in his hand.

"This reminds me of years ago when I did my own housework," Helen added as though it was a precious memory. She looked a lot younger wearing a pair of Missy's cutoffs.

Missy said, "I did rooms for three months at Lands End. People are slobs. The men spatter the toilet seat, and the women leave messes in the wastebasket."

"Some people," Helen corrected her.

"Do you think Jimmy's an alcoholic?" Helen asked a few minutes later when they'd worked their way into a corner.

"Everybody drinks," Missy said.

"Does he have blackouts?" Helen asked.

"You sound like a judge or something. I've only known him two months."

"But he shows you things he never shows me. He thinks he has to be good with me; he's always saying, 'I try to be good.' I tell him I don't want him to be good, but he doesn't know what I mean. I guess I've become his mother—that's what my therapist says."

"I don't believe in those people," Missy said.

"I have to go, for my daughter's sake," Helen said.

"You don't look much like a mom in that getup."

For the first time since daylight, Helen smiled. "Well, I have had my fill of mothering," she said. Then she went on, "If he's an alcoholic, he's suffering from a disease."

Missy wondered what the daughter looked like but Helen was still going on about drinking.

Missy said, "He feels better when he drinks. What's wrong with that?"

Helen handed her a sponge and got started on the counter. "I'm not judging him," she said. "That's not my responsibility. Why did they fire you at Miriam's?"

Missy sent the pink sponge flying across the counter. "The manager's a real prick. He was ragging on this black guy."

"And you objected?"

Missy nodded. "I heard a lot of that shit at home. For some reason I just can't stand it."

Helen stopped sponging and looked at her. "You are amazing," she said. She had that shine in her eyes.

Missy looked down at her sponge. "It isn't anything."

"Oh, but it is," Helen said.

"SADNESS WILL MAKE YOU DO THINGS," Missy explained next morning over croissants at The Hive, a golden-oak place on Duval Street that was full of people reading the *New York Times.*

"That's not the way I see it," Helen said. "Nothing can make me do something I don't want to."

"Did you choose to come down here, chasing me?"

"Yes," Helen said, and laughed.

"I don't believe it."

"How do you know so much?"

"I've lived," Missy said. And she told the story again about those fools on their knees outside the clinic. "Holding up these little plastic babies! At least I think they were plastic."

"That's terrible," Helen said. "I've sent money for Choice, of course, but I've never seen anything like that firsthand."

Missy loved her expressions.

She told Helen, "I sure as hell didn't want that baby. It wouldn't have been responsible," she added quickly, to cut off remembering how she had hung onto the nurse's hand while they sucked him out. She had known, even at six weeks, it was a boy.

"You have run the gamut," Helen said, and ordered more croissants. The breakfast was going to cost more than most dinners. Missy looked at the little golden oval pin Helen had clipped to the collar of her cotton dress.

"Promise me one thing," Helen went on after they had opened their croissants and put butter between the hot layers. "If it happens again, I mean, with Jimmy—"

"It won't, I had my tubes tied," Missy said. She knew what would come next, and she was having none of it.

LIGHT FROM THE STREET was coming in through rustling leaves, showing Missy her reflection in the mirrored walls of the bathroom. She thought she looked good in her bikini panties and nothing else. Her breasts were not large, which was something Jimmy liked; now that she had seen Helen's, she knew why. She held the gold pin to her nice deep navel and admired its flash.

"You took my pin," Helen said next morning.

"I'll give it back," Missy said. "I'm really sorry."

Helen began to cry.

"Oh shit," Missy said, and she reached out to pat her shoulder.

"It's not worth much—Jimmy couldn't afford then to buy me anything expensive," Helen said. "Oh God, why am I telling you this?"

"Because I'm your friend," Missy said, patting.

"Oh, no indeed. I have a lot of friends, I know something about the meaning—"

"I'll go right now and get it."

"Give me the house key first."

Missy fished the extra key out of the console drawer and gave it to Helen. "Say hello to Jimmy."

"I wouldn't dream of it," Helen said.

Missy opened the front door. Then she turned and reached for

Helen's solid hand. "I know you don't believe this right now, but I am your friend," she said.

"Oh, get out—please!"

WHEN MISSY FOUND HER, Lee Ann was not as nasty as she had expected. Missy explained she would only be staying for a few days, and Lee Ann felt sorry for her when she heard the story. She even loaned Missy some jeans and T-shirts to last her till she could get her clothes back.

Missy slept on and off for a couple of days. Key West in the rain was an ideal place to sleep. Jimmy was sure to be down for the weekend; it was nice to have a few days to rest, after what she'd been through.

On Thursday night while Lee Ann was working, Missy borrowed her bike and went over to the house on Simonton Street. The lights were off. She used her key to open the front door. Everything inside was shipshape; Helen had even arranged dried weeds in a jar on the mantel.

Missy went upstairs, turned on all the lights, and started to move her clothes back into the master bedroom. She made a little pile of stuff she didn't want, to pass on to Lee Ann. Jimmy always bought her something when he came down, and she had a hunch she'd get more than a T-shirt this time.

It was still raining and dark came on early, so she went to bed without bothering to fix anything to eat. She thought about changing the shell-pink sheets on the four-poster but felt too tired. Besides, she knew she would enjoy sleeping on those sheets; they still smelled of Helen's lavender perfume, over something drier and stranger.

David St. John

The Shore

So the tide forgets, as morning
Grows too far delivered, as the bowls
Of rock and wood run dry.
What is left seems pearled and lit,
As those cases
Of the museum stood lit
With milk jade, rows of opaque vases
Streaked with orange and yellow smoke.
You found a lavender boat, a single
Figure poling upstream, baskets
Of pale fish wedged between his legs.
Today, the debris of winter
Stands stacked against the walls,
The coils of kelp lie scattered
Across the floor. The oil fire
Smokes. You turn down the lantern
Hung on its nail. Outside,
The boats aligned like sentinels.
Here beside the blue depot, walking

The pier, you can see the way
The shore
Approximates the dream, how distances
Repeat their deaths
Above these tables and panes of water—
As climbing the hills above
The harbor, up to the lupine drifting
Among the lichen-masked pines,
The night is pocked with lamps lit
On every boat offshore,
Galleries of floating stars. Below,
On its narrow tracks shelved
Into the cliff's face,
The train begins its slide down
To the warehouses by the harbor. Loaded
With diesel, coal, paychecks, whiskey,
Bedsheets, slabs of ice—for the fish,
For the men. You lean on my arm,
As once
I watched you lean at the window;
The bookstalls below stretched a mile
To the quay, the afternoon crowd
Picking over the novels and histories.
You walked out as you walked out last
Night, onto the stone porch. Dusk
Reddened the walls, the winds sliced
Off the reefs. The vines of the gourds
Shook on their lattice. You talked
About that night you stood

Behind the black pane of the French
Window, watching my father read some long
Passage
Of a famous voyager's book. You hated
That voice filling the room,
Its light. So tonight we make a soft
Parenthesis upon the sand's black bed.
In that dream we share, there is
One shore, where we look out upon nothing
And the sea our whole lives;
Until turning from those waves, we find
One shore, where we look out upon nothing
And the earth our whole lives.
Where what is left between shore and sky
Is traced in the vague wake of
(The stars, the sandpipers whistling)
What we forgive. *If you wake soon, wake me.*

The Reef

The most graceful of misunderstandings
I could not keep close at hand
She paused a moment
At the door as she adjusted her scarf against
The winds & sprays & in the moonlight
She rowed back across the inlet to the shore

I sat alone above my pale vodka
Watching its smoky trails of peppercorns
Rising toward my lips

& while I flicked the radio dial
Trying to pick up the Cuban station or even
The static of "The Reggae Rooster" from Jamaica

I watched the waves foam above the coral & recede

Then foam breathlessly again & again
As a school of yellowtail
Rose together to the surface & then suddenly dove
Touched I knew by the long silver glove

Of the barracuda she loved to watch each afternoon
As she let the boat drift in its endlessly

Widening & broken arc

Peter Matthiessen

Under Montauk Light

In the early summer of 1954, a power boat with the most beautiful lines I had ever seen was riding at anchor in the harbor of Rockport, Massachusetts. Her designer turned out to be a local sailmaker who had built her as a tuna harpoon boat; she was the only one of her kind, and she was for sale. The following day I took the helm on a run around Cape Ann, as the owner ran forward to the pulpit and harpooned a small harbor seal (bountied in Massachusetts) with an astonishing throw of the clumsy pole. In Ipswich Bay, giant bluefin tuna were carving circles on the surface, and the sailmaker showed me how to approach them, how much to lead the swift fish on the throw, how important it was that everyone aboard stay well clear of the line tub when the fish was struck, but because he was selling his beautiful boat, he seemed too disheartened to pursue them.

With her high bow and deep hull forward, her long low cockpit and flat stern, the thirty-two foot boat looked like a trim and elegant Maine lobsterman, and she handled well in any kind of sea. Powered by a 120-horsepower Buick engine adapted to marine use (automobile engines, readily and cheaply acquired at wrecked-car yards, are often adapted by commercial fishermen), she came equipped with spotting tower, outriggers, harpoon stand, harpoons and line, a heavy tuna rod and reel and fighting chair, boat rods, shark hooks, and miscellaneous gear of all descriptions. At five thousand dollars, she was a bargain even in those days, and I knew from the first that she was my boat, though I had to borrow to obtain her; she was the most compulsive purchase of my life.

Signing the papers, the sailmaker was close to tears. He had designed and built this lovely craft with his own hands, he was losing her for an unworthy purpose (his wife desired a breezeway for their house), and throwing in all the fishing gear was an acknowledgment that a vital aspect of his life was at an end.

A few days later I ran the boat southward down the coast off Salem and Boston and on through the Cape Cod Canal and Buzzards Bay, putting in at Block Island late that evening, and continuing on to Three Mile Harbor the next day. By that time it had come to me, a little late, that writing and commercial fishing were barely paying my household expenses, that there was nothing left over for boat insurance, berth fees, maintenance, or even gas for a boat this size (the one-cylinder engine on my scallop boat ran mostly on air, and the rude hull could be berthed on a mud bank, invulnerable to theft or serious damage). And so, within a few days of her arrival, the beautiful boat I had rechristened *Merlin*—after the small swift falcon of that name as well as the celebrated magician—was sailing out of Montauk as a charter boat, with John Cole as mate. For the next two summers, often twice a day, we headed east along Gin Beach, rounding Shagwong Point and running south to join the fishing fleet off Montauk Point, or continuing offshore to the tuna grounds at the eighty-fathom line, where one misty morning of long and oily swells, many years before, I had seen the first whales of my life, the silver stream rising from the silver surface, the great dark shapes breaking the emptiness of ocean sky.

For many years as a boy in the late thirties, I had gone deep-sea fishing off Montauk with my father, and to this day I cannot see that high promontory of land with its historic lighthouse without a stirring of excitement and affection. Montauk is essentially a high rock island, cut off from the glacial moraines of the South Fork by a strait four miles wide. This strait, now filled with ocean sand, was known to the Indians as Napeague, or "water land"—old-timers speak of going "on" and "off" Montauk[1] as if it were still an island—and the headland at Montauk's eastern end was known to the Indians as Wompanon.[2] A lighthouse fired by sperm whale oil was constructed at Wompanon in 1795 by order of President George Washington, who proposed that it should stand for two hundred years.

Montauk's access to swift rips and deep ledges, to the wandering Gulf Stream, forty to seventy miles off to the south, has made it a legendary fishing place since Indian times. It was the fishing that attracted the developer Arthur Benson in 1879, when New York sportsmen were establishing striped bass fishing clubs in New York and Rhode Island. In 1880 some visionary anglers caused the construction of an iron fishing pier[3] over seven hundred feet long on the ocean beach at Napeague, only to see it torn away in its first winter.

Meanwhile, a small camp had been established at Fort Pond Bay by commercial fishermen from the North Fork. In the early 1880s, fishing was poor, and most of them transferred their operations to Rhode Island. Three years later, when the Rhode Island fishery declined, they returned to Montauk, finding the fish "more plentiful than was ever known before."

Then, at the turn of the century, a William J. Morgan, surfcasting under the Light, landed a seventy-six-pound striped bass that made Montauk famous. Wherever this hero went thereafter, it was said, people would point and say, "That's Morgan!" But Morgan was no doubt well aware of the 101-pound specimen taken off East Hampton in this period by Nathaniel Dominy's haul-seine crew. Cap'n Dominy laid the monster out in style in a farm wagon and trundled it around East Hampton and Sag Harbor, charging the villagers ten cents each for a good look before selling it for five dollars to a Sag Harbor hotel; no doubt people draw breath today whose forebears dined on that historic fish. The obsessed Morgan, who tried for the rest of his life to catch one larger, built a house on Montauk overlooking a surfcasting site that was known as "Morgan's" for decades thereafter.

Within a few years of the arrival of the railroad in 1895—and despite Montauk's meager population and facilities—the fishing community at Fort Pond Bay became the principal fish shipping port on the East End, with hundreds of tons of black sea bass and other species shipped every day. Tracks were built onto the dock for a special fish train that was loaded directly from the boats. It left Montauk at 4:30 P.M., picked up boxes of fish at the depot platform known as Fanny Bartlett's, or Napeague Station, as well as at Amagansett and East Hampton, and arrived in the New York markets before daylight.

For years to come there was no paved road across the sands of Napeague,[4] and Montauk's shantytown of fishermen and fish packers remained clustered on the eastern shore of Fort Pond Bay, with four or five pioneer summer cottages on the dunes opposite. Mrs. Agnew's Tea Room was the only building on the wagon road between the settlement and Montauk Light. The fishing community, notably the Parsons, Edwards, and Hulse families from Amagansett and the large Tuthill clan from Orient and East Marion on the North Fork, in addition to some people from Connecticut, would usually arrive in early May and go home in fall; most of them lived in simple shacks constructed from "fish box boards"—the big sugar boxes, made from sugar pine, that would carry ten bushels of skimmers or six hundred pounds of fish. Since Fort Pond Bay was relatively unprotected, the fishing boats were moored to spiles, or stakes, offshore that were limber enough to bend with the strong winds. The Parsonses and Tuthills ran their own boats and kept their own fish houses on the east shore of the bay; the fishing company on the south shore belonged to J. C. Wells.

The Edwards Brothers, running ocean traps off Amagansett, unloaded their catch at the Tuthill dock. In early April, four to ten ocean traps, or barrel traps—a leader or wing turned fish offshore into a series of funnels and pens—were set up to a mile offshore in about seven fathoms of water, to catch whatever came along in the strong spring run. The ocean trap was similar in design to a large pound trap but used anchors instead of stakes. A crew of forty, in four seine boats, was required to lift these traps, from which twelve tons or more of edible fish might be harvested each day. When the ocean traps were taken up, about June 1, the crews were switched to the big bunker steamers, which sailed from the Edwards Brothers docks near the menhaden factories (called Bunker City) now concentrated in the vicinity of Promised Land, west of Napeague Harbor. In the twenties, the Tuthills and Jake Wells hired summer help from Nova Scotia to work in the packing houses and on the docks, and some of these men moved down to Promised Land to crew on the Edwards Brothers boats. A Montauk colony of Nova Scotia families—including such fishing clans as the Pittses and Beckwiths—are part of the Montauk community to this day.

Most of the early Montauk fishermen were trappers, and the Tuthills lifted their fish pounds, or traps, on Gardiners Island as well as in the environs of Fort Pond Bay. On a map made early in the century, nearly three hundred traps are shown between North Bar at Montauk Point and Eastern Plains Point on Gardiners Island, a far denser concentration than exists today.[5] Captain Nat Edwards, son of Cap'n Gabe, ran a dozen pound traps between Shagwong Point and Water Fence; Captain Sam Edwards and other fishermen ran small low-powered draggers, thirty to thirty-five feet long, or set lobster pots, or hand-lined for pollock, sea bass, and bluefish.

THROUGHOUT THE HAMPTONS, small scallop boats and other craft had been catering to summer fishing parties since the turn of the century. Montauk draggermen did well with swordfish (by August 7 in the summer of 1925, Captain George Beckwith had harpooned thirty-seven) and in the late twenties and early thirties, when Montauk was developed as a resort, many draggers joined the early charter fleet. In 1927 the first swordfish ever taken on rod and reel was brought into Fort Pond Bay by one of the Florida fishing guides drawn to the area. The following year the former Great Pond, rechristened Lake Montauk, was permanently opened to the bay, creating an all-weather harbor.

In the mid-twenties, when agitation to restrict the activities of commercial men had already started, a federal hatchery for production of lobster, codfish, flounder, and pollock was proposed for Fort Pond Bay, and a freezing plant designed to market prepacked fish was already under construction. But these enterprises were abandoned with the opening and development of Great Pond. Although certain old-timers stuck to Fort Pond Bay for another twenty years, the construction of additional docks, and the protected anchorage, had drawn most of the fleet to the new harbor. The Napeague road was long since paved, and the fish train was now replaced by truckers. Commercial men such as Gus and Fred Pitts (of the Nova Scotia colony), draggermen Dan Grimshaw and Harry Conklin (who took out President Herbert Hoover), and the Beckwith, Erickson, and Tuma brothers soon adapted their work boats for chartering; even Captains Sam and Bert Edwards, and later Sam's sons Kenneth and Dick, took time off from bunkering to join the fleet. Before long, big bottom-fishing boats were developed that would attract thousands of people to Montauk every year. More than five thousand customers were recorded in 1932, and this number tripled the following year and doubled again in 1934, when the Long Island Rail Road established daily excursion trains from New York and Brooklyn. S. Kip Farrington of East Hampton (ignoring the surfmen) described the pioneer fish guides of the thirties as the rightful heirs of Captain Josh Edwards and the shore whalers; as a big game fisherman and sport-fishing writer, he did more to advertise the new craze for deep-sea fishing than anyone else before or since. By the mid-thirties, special deep-sea fishing boats with twin screw engines and flying bridges had been designed for working the Gulf Stream, sometimes as far as seventy miles offshore; the fish prized most were swordfish, marlin, and the giant bluefin tuna, moving north and south from its summer grounds off Wedgeport, Nova Scotia.

The 1938 hurricane created the Shinnecock Inlet, now a fishing station, but it mostly destroyed the Montauk fishing village at Fort Pond Bay. The railroad depot is still there, however, and so is the fish company founded by E. D. Tuthill and owned today by Perry Duryea, Jr., whose father married Captain Ed Tuthill's daughter. The hundreds of boats that once littered the bay are now in Montauk Harbor, which by the time of my arrival in the early fifties was already home port for one of the largest sport-fishing fleets on the East Coast.

That summer of 1954, the charter season was well under way when the *Merlin* arrived. There was one slip left at the town dock, right across from one of the pioneer charter men, John Messbauer, and we soon found out why nobody had wanted it; the current was strong and the approach narrow, and the one way to back a single-engine boat into this berth was a sequence of swirling maneuvers at full throttle. Unless executed with precision, these maneuvers would strand the boat across the bows of neighboring boats, held fast by the current, while the customers wondered how their lives had been consigned to such lubberly hands. Before I got the hang of it, there was more than one humiliating episode, not helped by the embarrassment of my trusty mate, who would shrug, wince, and roll his eyes, pretending to the old salts along the dock that if only this greenhorn would let him take the helm, he could do much better.

At thirty-two feet, the *Merlin* was small by Montauk standards, and she lacked the customary flying bridge, not to mention upholstered fighting chairs, teak decks, and chrome. We had no old customers to depend on, and no big shiny cockpit to attract new ones, and Captain Al Ceslow on the *Skip II,* for whom John had worked as mate the previous summer, was the only man in the whole fleet of forty-five-odd boats who would offer advice or help of any kind. However, it was soon July, and fish and fishing parties both abounded (and were biting hard, said cynical Jimmy Reutershan, who was bluefishing out of Montauk in his Jersey skiff, and who believed strongly in lunar tide tables as a guide to the feeding habits of fish and man; he had noticed, he said, that *Homo sapiens,* wandering the docks with a glazed countenance, would suddenly stir into feeding frenzy, signing up boats with the same ferocity—and at the same stage of the tide—that *Pomatomus saltatrix* would strike into the lures around the Point).

And so, from the first, the *Merlin* did pretty well. We made up in eagerness and love of fishing what we lacked in experience of our new trade, we worked hard to find fish for our clients, and except on weekends, when we ran two six-hour trips each day, we sailed overtime without extra charge whenever the morning had been unproductive. Also, unlike many of the charter men, who seemed to feel that anglers of other races belonged on "barf barges"—the party or bottom-fishing boats—we welcomed anyone who came along. One day we sailed a party of Chinese laundrymen from up-Island, each one equipped with a full-sized galvanized garbage can. Their one recognizable utterance was "Babylon." Conveying to us through their Irish-American interpreter that trolling for hard-fighting and abundant bluefish did not interest them, they said that they wished to be taken to the three coal barges sunk southwest of the Point in a nor'easter, a well-known haunt of the black sea bass so highly esteemed in Chinese cookery. Once the hulks were located, they set out garbage cans along the cockpit and pin-hooked sea bass with such skill (to cries of "Bobby-lon!") that every man topped off his garbage can. The half ton of sea bass that they took home more than paid the cost of the whole charter, while gladdening every Oriental heart in western Suffolk.

Another day, three Shinnecock Indian chiefs in quest of "giants" (they were soon off to Alaska, they declared, to shoot giant brown bear) took us all the way to Rosie's Hole off the coast of Rhode Island in vain pursuit of giant bluefin. Because of the fuel, the barrel of bunker chum bought at Ted's freezer, and the installation of the *Merlin*'s heavy tuna chair, the trip was expensive even for car dealers from Washington, D.C., where the three chiefs spent most of the year, passing themselves off as black men. The chiefs liked us because the other boats had refused their trade, and we liked them because they spent their money cheerfully, though they saw neither hide nor hair of giants.

No other boat got a bluefin that day either, and John and I were relieved as well as disappointed; in theory, we knew what to do once the huge fish took the mackerel bait that we drifted down the current (crank up the engine, cast off the buoy on the anchor, and chase after the exhilarated fish before it stripped the last line off the reel), but being inexperienced with giant tuna, we foresaw all sorts of possibilities for dangerous error. Big bluefin may be ten feet long, and nearly a half ton in weight, and the speed and power of these fish are awesome. (In the *Merlin*'s former life in Ipswich Bay, a passenger had come too close to the blur of green line leaving the tub after a horse mackerel had been harpooned. The line whipped around his leg and snapped him overboard and down thirty feet under the sea before someone grabbed a hatchet and whacked the line where it sizzled across the brass strip on the combing. Had that hatchet not been handy, and wits quick, the nosy passenger would have lost his life.)

Toward the end of the homeward journey across Block Island Sound, I encouraged the chiefs to stop on Shagwong Reef and pick up a few bluefish to take home for supper. The thwarted giant-killers had consoled themselves with gin on the long voyage, and one man agreed to fish for blues if we would strap him into the big fighting chair and give him that thick tuna rod to work with, so that he could imagine what it must be like to deal masterfully with one of those monsters back at Rosie's Hole. When the strike came, it failed to bend even the rod tip, but the angler, cheered on by his friends, set the hook with a mighty backward heave into the fighting chair. "It's charging the boat!" his assistants yelled as something broke the surface; the only porgy in the *Merlin*'s history that ever went for a trolled bluefish lure had been snapped clear out of the water by that heave and skimmed through the air over the wake in a graceful flight that a flying fish might well have envied.

So much did all three chiefs enjoy this exciting fishing experience that they felt obliged to lie down in the cockpit, collapsed with laughter. "No mo' bluefishin," they cried helplessly, waving us on. "Giant pogie's good enough!" Once ashore, they gave both of us giant tips, thanked us as "scholars and gentlemen" for a splendid outing, and went off merrily down the dock with their souvenir porgy. Next time they visited these parts, they said, they would bring their girlfriends down to meet us (which they did).

Not all our clients were such good sports as the three chiefs. A charter demands six hours at close quarters with company that is rarely of one's choice, and often there are two charters each day. While most of our people were cooperative and pleasant, others felt that their money entitled them to treat captain and mate as servants, and one ugly customer advised me even before the *Merlin* cleared the breakwater that he knew all about the charter men's tricks and cheating ways. I turned the boat around, intending to put him on the dock, but his upset friends made him apologize.

Another day the motor broke down on Shagwong Reef in clear, rough weather of a northwest wind. A cockpit full of queasy passengers wanted to know why I did not call the Coast Guard. The truth was that their captain, having had no time to go to New York and apply to the Coast Guard for a captain's license, was running a renegade boat, and was stalling for time until Al Ceslow on the *Skip II* could finish his morning charter and tow us in. One of the men, under the horrified gaze of his newlywed wife, actually panicked, shrieking at the other passengers that the captain's plan was to put this death craft on the rocks; I had to grab him by the shirtfront and bang him up against the cabinside to calm him down. (On another charter boat one morning—we could hear the shouts and crashing right over the radio-telephone—a disgruntled client had to be slugged into submission, with the skipper bellowing for police assistance at the dock.)

The *Merlin* was plagued by persistent hazing from two charter boats that now and then would turn across our wake, out on the Elbow, and cut off all four of our wire lines; no doubt other new boats were welcomed in this way as well. Wire lines, lures, and leaders are expensive, and because wire line is balky stuff, it often took most of an hour of good fishing tide to re-rig the lines for the unhappy customers. The two big captains of these big boats (both of them sons of earlier big captains who now ran big enterprises on the docks) were successful charter men who had nothing to fear from the small *Merlin*; often this pair trolled side by side, chatting on radio-telephones from their flying bridges. One day off Great Eastern Rock,[6] heart pounding with mixed fear and glee, and deaf to all oaths and shouts of warning, I spun my wheel and cut across both of their fat sterns, taking all eight of their wire lines at a single blow.

In the long stunned silence on all three boats, John Cole said quietly, "Oh boy," and suggested a long detour to Connecticut. "Those guys are going to be waiting for us on the dock," he said, "and they are BIG." But there was no reception party, and our lines were never cut again. Not long thereafter one of these skippers called the *Merlin* on "the blower," passing terse word in the charter man's way that he was into fish: "See where we are, Cap, down to the east'rd? Better come this way."

One day on the ocean side, working in close to the rocks west of the Light, we picked up a striped bass on the inshore line and a bluefish on the outside; we did this on three straight passes, and probably could have done it again if we had not been late for our afternoon charter and had to head in. So far as we knew, those three bass, and three more the next day from the same place, were the only stripers taken out of Montauk for nearly a fortnight in the bass dog days of late July. From that day on, we had to wait to fish this spot until the fleet went in at noon, because other boats began to tail us with binoculars, in the same way that the *Merlin* sometimes tailed Gus Pitts when the *Marie II* worked the striper holes along the beach, watching his mate strip out the wire to guess the depth at which Cap'n Gus was trolling, or glimpse what lure he was rigging to his rods.

On days when we had no charter, we went out hand-lining for blues, heading west past Culloden Point[7] and Fort Pond Bay to Water Fence, at the western boundary of the land acquired by the Proprietors of Montauk, where the cattle fence that once kept East Hampton's livestock on the Montauk pastures during the summer had extended out into the water; past the walking dunes, a sand flow at the old forest edge on the north side of Hither Hills; past Goff Point and the fallen chimney of the abandoned bunker factory at Hicks Island.[8] East of Cartwright Shoal, the shallow waters teemed with small three-pound "tailor" bluefish that bit as fast as the hand lines were tossed overboard, and brought a good price on the market.[9]

The *Merlin* was no longer a renegade boat (I got my license in late summer), and no one ignored her radio queries or disdained to call her; she had already built up a list of clients who wished to charter her again the following year. The bluefishing was strong and steady, and offshore the school tuna were so thick that by leaving one fish on the line while boating the other three, we could keep all four lines loaded almost continually until the box had overflowed. On some days, poor John, skidding around on the bloody deck, exhausted from pumping the strong tuna off the bottom for the weary customers, would send me wild-eyed signals to get the boat away from the goddamn fish, maybe show the clients a nice shark or ocean sunfish.

But there were days in that first summer when the *Merlin* sat idle at the dock, and in August the price of bluefish was so low that hand-lining would not make us a day's pay. Bass remained scarce in the dead of summer, and one morning when his boat was hauled out for repairs, we decided to show our friend Al Ceslow our secret striper spot on the ocean shore west of the Light.

In the days before, there had been offshore storms, and the big smooth swells collapsing on the coast would make it difficult to work close to the rocks. We also knew that Cap'n Gus, widely regarded as the best striped bass fisherman ever to sail under the Light, had put three boats on those rocks in his twenty years of hard experience. And so we rode in as close as we dared on the backs of the broad waves, letting the lures coast in on the white wash. We were not close enough, and tried to edge in closer, keeping an eye out for the big freak sea that would break offshore and wash us onto the rock shore under the cliffs. Unlike the established boats, we were not booked solid a full year in advance, and the loss of the *Merlin*—we could not yet afford insurance—would mean the end of our careers as charter boatmen, apart from endangering our lives.

The wave we feared rose up behind us, sucking the water off the inshore rocks, and as Al or John shouted, I spun the wheel and gave the *Merlin* her full throttle. With a heavy thud, our trusty boat struck into the midsection of a high, clear, cresting wave, and for one sickening moment, seemed to lose headway. Then the wave parted, two walls of green water rushed past the cockpit, over our heads, and the boat sprang up and outward, popping free. If we ever fished that spot again, I do not recall it.

HURRICANE CAROL, on the last day of August 1954, blew so hard at Montauk that I ran the Merlin at eight knots in her slip in order to ease the pressure on her lines. At high water, only the spile tops on the town dock were visible above the flood, which carried loose boats and capsized hulks down toward the breakwater. In leaping from the stern to fetch more lines or lend a hand with another boat, one could only pray that the town dock was still there.

The hurricane's eye passed over about noon, in an eerie silver light and sulfurous pall. Then the winds struck in again, subsiding only as our fuel ran low in midafternoon. By evening we felt free to leave for home, but could not get there; the storm seas, surging through the dunes, had reopened the old strait in a new channel into Napeague Harbor, knocking down one of the radio towers that transmitted to the ships at sea. Until late that night, when the tide turned and the sea subsided, we were stranded on Montauk, which was once again an island.

I was not sorry when the season was over and I ran my boat back west to Three Mile Harbor. To judge from the sour, contemptuous remarks that were traded back and forth on the radio-telephones, a lot of charter men were opportunists, out for an easy dollar that was not forthcoming. Almost all of us made good money between July 4 and Labor Day, but only the best boats in the fleet, with the longest lists of faithful customers (these were the charter captains we admired, the skilled and happy ones who loved to fish) could make it in the colder days of spring and autumn. The *Merlin* was not yet one of those boats, and we quit right after Labor Day, to make the most of the first weeks of the scallop season. It was a poor season that year, with so many scallops destroyed by Hurricane Carol.

The *Merlin*'s summer in 1955 was busy and successful, but I ended my second year of chartering with the same feeling. I chartered because it paid for my boat and I made a living out of doors in the season between haul-seining and scalloping; I scalloped and hauled seine because I liked the work, and liked the company of the commercial fishermen, the baymen.

NOTES

1 Old-timers pronounce Montauk with an accented second syllable.

2 From the Algonkian *Wapaneunk*, "to the east."

3 The iron pier had a fish trap at the end.

4 During World War I, the Long Island Rail Road laid a cinder track parallel to its own roadbed, south of the old sand track, and this cinder track was paved in the late nineteen twenties.

5 In 1984 there were fifty-three traps in East Hampton Town, from Culloden Point to Northwest Harbor, and about ten on the shores of Gardiners Island.

6 A rock needle twenty-four feet below the surface, discovered the hard way by the iron ship *Great Eastern* that later laid the first trans-Atlantic cable.

7 In 1781 the 161-foot British gunboat *Culloden*, after striking on Shagwong Reef, sank under the bluffs of Fort Pond Bay.

8 Off this Napeague shore, the slave ship *Amistad*, in 1839, commandeered by its cargo under the leadership of an extraordinary African named Cinque, was taken in custody by the revenue brig *Washington*, thereby precipitating a political crisis and an epochal decision by the U.S. Supreme Court in the national conflict over abolition that would lead in a few years to civil war.

9 In Australia, all bluefish are called tailors, pronounced "tie-lers," apparently an old English term, still used locally for two- to three-pound bluefish.

James Harms

Decadence:
Newport Beach, California

Sure it's bright, a good day by some standards.
A child staggers past on plastic skates
still stepping instead of rolling,
oblivious to her own blonde hair

exploding in the wind,
to the crowd of joggers piling up
behind her, who run in place
and check their watches as if

her balance is their custody,
a crystal vase they must carry
for the time it takes her
to work out this new knowledge.

Another kid plays with a sail on the beach,
gets tangled up in canvas
on the slim strip of sand.
He looks like a tiny mummy, but no one's watching

so no one's scared, except him:
he fears the tide's soft fingers,
the Christmas lights floating in the sticky water, a plastic
wine glass, a strand of kelp. And it's hard to breathe.

Such a long list of fears, really,
for one so young.
And Larry the can man can't stand it,
Larry the can man

who owns this particular route,
who is screaming about the noise the sun is making
and he's got a point: it's hard to hear the light
dancing on the water with all this glare.

So when the century ends instead of the world
and we sip our last beers on the pier,
the strange gold light
like dust on the water. . . .

And there she goes, a woman tan beyond beauty
somewhat drunk and smiling;
she walks off the dock as if feigning disgrace.
In all the confusion,

her infant son crawls away
and finds the abandoned sail, lifts it up, disappears.
While around us the houses huddle
in the wind, which tears the sun

from the little skater's hair
and rips the harbor into pieces
chips of light between the boats
like bottle glass on broken pavement.

Larry wails for broken bottles
but he's seeing things,
he's looking right at us. No.
It's the ocean over our shoulders; he's looking at that.

Elegy as Evening, as Exodus

North of Malibu

The Pacific is nothing like its name.
For one thing, there are no silences,
despite the palm trees leaning into stillness.

Poppies rise like fire from the chaparral
on the bluffs, the manzanita, the oil in its leaves.
And every few yards a stubborn yucca,

late blossoms struggling to catch up at the edge
of whatever, this modern earth, tectonic rafts
slipping north and west, the ocean torn into white lace.

Tan knees tucked beneath my chin,
tan knees like a boy's, I sat watch
through the afternoon, staring at the islands:

Anacapa, San Miguel, Catalina to the south.
I heard a phone ring, a buoy bell, sun dissolving
into sea. I heard a name escape its word,

the wind between waves. The islands were rose and gray
in the last light of a last Tuesday,
the rock around me dark and trembling, volcanic.

I sat in the splash zone, black urchins
tucked into wet crevices at my feet,
a keyhole limpet next to my left hand.

And though you would suppose the islands
would vanish into the channel when the sun did,
for hours I could see their shapes, like whales

sleeping peacefully on the horizon,
like ships. Ships waiting for enough light,
for safe passage, for cargo. For all of us.

The Hole in the Moon

I'm walking home wishing I was someone else,
and it's Sunday on the beach so everywhere I look
there are possibilities.
The moon's been funny this week, anchovies
are running the surf. People wade in
with nets and wire baskets, one boy
carries a cardboard box, but everybody
walks off with bait to sell or salt away.
Waves throw fish against the sand
and the shimmering is awful, the beach littered
for miles with little twitches of light.

Last night I was walking home
and stopped to watch some men string lights
from their car batteries to play basketball.
I hooked my fingers in the chainlink
and stood there while they shot around
then started playing.
But I was thinking about the Korean families
down for the day fishing, and the little girl
I'd seen earlier tugging a sandshark toward a bucket.
So when one guy dropped the ball
and swung at his friend, I went home

and slept, woke-up and went to breakfast
at RUBY'S-On-the-Pier. Now these anchovies
all over the beach, kids screaming
or their parents screaming.

It's not like I hate it, but I do.
On a Wednesday in March
I sat here with you, not a sandwich
in sight. The air was quiet and clear,
and Catalina seemed close enough to touch,
like we could walk to it. I bet today

we could, on the backs of all these fish;
if you were here I think we'd try.
So I sit and wish for that, and for this tide
to drop. I guess, really, I'm wishing for something less,
a hole in the moon maybe, and from it
a small pill of hope. But I don't say anything.
I just close my eyes like I always did,
like someone who's trying to remember,
and place you nearby
where, by chance, I might be going.

Terri Ford

The Beach of My Mom

I know why the ships are she. I've got
this parent, striding down shore
like she means it. She does, swinging heads
of iceberg lettuce, purple cabbage. My mom
is a team, she's the strength
of blue, told off the Christmas tree
the year my dad left.

My mom is taking things out of my hands
to improve me. "Just *tell* me how," I say—apple pie,
hammer, needle—but she hasn't the words, asks
for the whatzit sitting on the thing
over there. This is how
she's always loved me—nonspecific, standing
too close like a basketball forward
in the too bright light, trying to take
the ball meant for mine, so when I look up
my moments of light are obscured by a reaching

of arms and a holler and all of the vast trees
are calling to me lest I injure myself, which I do.

My mother's not sleeping. She says
it's her change; for years she's charted every
outbreak: light spotting, old rust; or floating, how
she woke up drenched. She is endless, the beach
of my mom. I came from this
roaring. Against this current I'm wading out.

Charles D'Ambrosio, Jr.

The Point

I had been lying awake after my nightmare, a nightmare in which Father and I bought helium balloons at a circus. I tied mine around my finger and Father tied his around a stringbean and lost it. After that, I lay in the dark, tossing and turning, sleepless from all the sand in my sheets and all the uproar out in the living room. Then the door opened, and for a moment the blade of bright light blinded me. The party was still going full blast, and now with the door ajar and my eyes adjusting I glimpsed the silver smoke swirling in the light and all the people suspended in it, hovering around as if they were angels in heaven—some kind of heaven where the host serves highballs and the men smoke cigars and the women all smell like rotting fruit. Everything was hysterical out there—the men laughing, the ice clinking, the women shrieking. A woman crossed over and sat on the edge of my bed, bending over me. It was Mother. She was backlit, a vague, looming silhouette, but I could smell lily of the valley and something else—lemon rind from the bitter twist she always chewed when she reached the watery bottom of her vodka-and-tonic. When Father was alive, she rarely drank, but after he shot himself you could say she really let herself go.

"Dearest?" she said.

"Hi, Mom," I said.

"Your old mother's bombed, dearest—flat-out bombed."

"That's O.K.," I said. She liked to confess these things to me, although it was always obvious how tanked she was, and I never cared. I considered myself a pro at this business. "It's a party," I said, casually. "Live it up."

"Oh, God," she laughed. "I don't know how I got this way."

"What do you want, Mom?"

"Yes, dear," she said. "There was something I wanted."

She looked out the window—at the sail-white moon beyond the black branches of the apple tree—and then she looked into my eyes. "What was it I wanted?" Her eyes were moist, and mapped with red veins. "I came here for a reason," she said, "but I've forgotten it now."

"Maybe if you go back you'll remember," I suggested.

Just then, Mrs. Gurney leaned through the doorway. "Well?" she said, slumping down on the floor. Mrs. Gurney had bright-silver hair and a dark tan—the sort of tan that women around here get when their marriages start busting up. I could see the gaudy gold chains looped around Mrs. Gurney's dark-brown neck winking in the half-light before they plunged from sight into the darker gulf between her breasts.

"That's it," Mother said. "Mrs. Gurney. She's worse off than me. She's really blitzo. Blotto? Blitzed?"

"Hand me my jams," I said.

I slipped my swim trunks on underneath the covers.

For years I'd been escorting these old inebriates over the sandy playfield and along the winding boardwalks and up the salt-whitened steps of their homes, brewing coffee, fixing a little toast or heating leftovers, searching the medicine cabinets for aspirin and vitamin B, setting a glass of water on the nightstand, or the coffee table if they'd collapsed on the couch—and even, once, tucking some old fart snugly into bed between purple silk sheets. I'd guide these drunks home and hear stories about the alma mater, Theta Xi, Boeing stock splits, Cadillacs, divorce, Nembutal, infidelity, and often the people I helped home gave me three or four bucks for listening to all their sad business. I suppose it was better than a paper route. Father, who'd been a medic in Vietnam, made it my job when I was ten, and at thirteen I considered myself a hard-core veteran, treating every trip like a mission.

"O.K., Mrs. Gurney," I said. "Upsy-daisy."

She held her hand out, and I grabbed it, leaned back, and hoisted her to her feet. She stood there a minute, listing this way, that way, like a sailor who hadn't been to port in a while.

Mother kissed her wetly on the lips and then said to me, "Hurry home."

"I'm toasted," Mrs. Gurney explained. "Just toasted."

"Let's go out the back way," I said. It would only take longer if we had to navigate our way through the party, offering excuses and making those ridiculous promises adults always make to one another when the party's over. "Hey, we'll do it again," they assure each other, as if that needed to be said. And I'd noticed how, with the summer ending and Labor Day approaching, all the adults would acquire a sort of desperate, clinging manner, as if this were all going to end forever, and the good times would never be seen again. Of course I now realize that the end was just an excuse to party like maniacs. The softball tournament, the salmon derby, the cocktails, the clambakes, the barbecues, would all happen again. They always had and they always would.

Anyway, out the back door and down the steps.

Once I'd made a big mistake with a retired account executive, a friend of Father's. Fred was already falling-down drunk, so it didn't help at all that he had two more drinks on the way out the door, apologizing for his condition, which no one noticed, and boisterously offering bad stock tips. I finally got Fred going and dragged him partway home in a wagon, dumping his fat ass in front of his house— close enough, I figured—wedged in against some driftwood so the tide wouldn't wash him out to sea. He didn't get taken out to sea, but the sea did come to him, as the tide rose, and when he woke he was lassoed in green kelp. Fortunately, he'd forgotten the whole thing— how he'd got where he was, where he'd been before that—but it scared me that a more or less right-hearted attempt on my part might end in such an ugly mess.

By now, though, I'd worked this job so long I knew all the tricks.

THE MOON WAS FULL and immaculately white in a blue-black sky. The wind funneled down Saratoga Passage, blowing hard, blowing south, and Mrs. Gurney and I were struggling against it, tacking back and forth across the playfield. Mrs. Gurney strangled her arm around my neck and we wobbled along. Bits of sand shot in our eyes and blinded us.

"Keep your head down, Mrs. Gurney! I'll guide you!"

She plopped herself down in the sand, nesting there as if she were going to lay an egg. She unbuckled her sandals and tossed them behind her. I ran back and fetched them from the sand. Her skirt fluttered in the wind and flew up in her face. Her silver hair, which was usually shellacked with spray and coiffed to resemble a crash helmet, cracked and blew apart, splintering like a clutch of straw.

"Why'd I drink so damned much?" she screamed. "I'm toasted—

really, Kurt, I'm totally toasted. I shouldn't have drunk so damned much."

"Well, you did, Mrs. Gurney," I said, bending toward her. "That's not the problem now. The problem now is how to get you home."

"Why, God damn it!"

"Trust me, Mrs. Gurney. Home is where you want to be."

One tip about these drunks: My opinion is that it pays in the long run to stick as close as possible to the task at hand. We're just going home, you assure them, and tomorrow it will all be different. I've found if you stray too far from the simple goal of getting home and going to sleep, you let yourself in for a lot of unnecessary hell. You start hearing about their whole miserable existence, and suddenly it's the most important thing in the world to fix it all up, right then. Certain things in life can't be repaired, as in Father's situation, and that's always sad, but I believe there's nothing in life that can be remedied under the influence of half a dozen planter's punches.

Now, not everyone on the Point was a crazed rumhound, but the ones that weren't, the people who accurately assessed their capacities and balanced their intake accordingly, the people who never got lost, who never passed out in flower beds or, adrift in the maze of narrow boardwalks, gave up the search for home altogether and walked into any old house that was nearby—they, the people who never did these things and knew what they were about, never needed my help. They also weren't too friendly with my mother and didn't participate in her weekly bashes. The Point was kind of divided that way—between the upright, seaworthy residents and the easily overturned friends of my mother's.

Mrs. Gurney lived about a half-mile up the beach in a bungalow with a lot of Gothic additions. The scuttlebutt on Mrs. Gurney was that while she wasn't divorced, her husband didn't love her. This kind of knowledge was part of my job, something I didn't relish but accepted as an occupational hazard. I knew all the gossip, the rumors, the rising and falling fortunes of my mother's friends. After a summer, I'd have the dirt on everyone, whether I wanted it or not. But I had developed a priestly sense of my position, and whatever anyone told me in a plastered, blathering confessional fit was as safe and privileged as if it had been spoken in a private audience with the Pope. Still, I hoped Mrs. Gurney would stick to the immediate goal and not start talking about how sad and lonely she was, or how cruel her husband was, or what was going to become of us all, etc.

The wind rattled the swings back and forth, chains creaking, and whipped the ragged flag, which flew at half-mast. Earlier that summer, Mr. Crutchfield, the insurance lawyer, had fallen overboard and drowned while hauling in his crab trap. He always smeared his bait box with Mentholatum, which is illegal, and the crabs went crazy for it, and I imagined that in his greed, catching over the limit, he couldn't haul the trap up but wouldn't let go, either, and the weight pulled him into the sea, and he had a heart attack and drowned. The current floated him all the way to Everett before he was found, white and bloated as soggy bread.

Mrs. Gurney was squatting on the ground, lifting fistfuls of sand and letting them course through her fingers, the grains falling away as through an hourglass.

"Mrs. Gurney? We're not making much progress."

She rose to her feet, gripping my pant leg, my shirt, my sleeve, then my neck. We started walking again. The sand was deep and loose, and with every step we sank down through the soft layers until a solid purchase was gained in the hard-packed sand below, and we could push off in baby steps. The night was sharp, and alive with shadows—everything, even the tiny tufted weeds that sprouted through the sand, had a shadow—and this deepened the world, made it seem thicker, with layers, and more layers, and then a darkness into which I couldn't see.

"You know," Mrs. Gurney said, "the thing about these parties is, the thing about drinking is—you know, getting so damnably blasted is . . ." She stopped, and tried to mash her wild hair back down into place, and, no longer holding on to anything other than her head, fell back on her ass into the sand.

I waited for her to finish her sentence, then gave up, knowing it was gone forever. Her lipstick, I noticed, was smeared clownishly around her mouth, fixing her lips into a frown, or maybe a smirk. She smelled different from my mother—like pepper, I thought, and bananas. She was taller than me, and a little plump, with a nose shaped exactly like her head, like a miniature replica of it right in the middle of her face.

We finally got off the playfield and onto the boardwalk that fronted the seawall. A wooden wagon leaned over in the sand. I tipped it upright.

"Here you go, Mrs. Gurney," I said, pointing to the wagon. "Hop aboard."

"I'm O.K.," she protested. "I'm fine. Fine and dandy."

"You're not fine, Mrs. Gurney."

The caretaker built these wagons out of old hatches from P.T. boats. They were heavy, monstrous, and made to last. Once you got them rolling, they cruised.

Mrs. Gurney got in, not without a good deal of operatics, and when I finally got her to shut up and sit down I started pulling. I'd never taken her home before, but on a scale of one to ten, ten being the most obstreperous, I was rating her about a six at this point.

She stretched out like Cleopatra floating down the Nile in her barge. "Stop the world," she sang, "I want to get off."

I vaguely recalled that as a song from my parents' generation. It reminded me of my father, who shot himself in the head one morning—did I already say this? He was sitting in the grass parking lot above the Point. Officially, his death was ruled an accident, a "death by misadventure," and everyone believed that he had in fact been cleaning his gun, but Mother told me otherwise one night. Mother had a batch of lame excuses she tried on me, but it only made me sad to see her groping for an answer and falling way short. I wished she'd come up with something, just for herself. Father used to say that everyone up here was *dinky dow*, which is Vietnamese patois for "crazy." At times, after Father died, I thought Mother was going a little *dinky dow* herself.

I leaned forward, my head bent against the wind. Off to starboard, the sea was black, with a line of moonlit white waves continually crashing on the shore. Far off, I could see the dark headlands of Hat Island, the island itself rising from the water like a breaching whale, and then, beyond, the soft, blue, irresolute lights of Everett, on the distant mainland.

I stopped for a breather, and Mrs. Gurney was gone. She was sitting on the boardwalk, a few houses back.

"Look at all these houses," Mrs. Gurney said, swinging her arms around.

"Let's go, Mrs. Gurney."

"Another fucking great summer at the Point."

The wind seemed to be refreshing Mrs. Gurney, but that was a hard one to call. Often drunks seemed on the verge of sobering up, and then, just as soon as they got themselves nicely balanced, they plunged off the other side, into depression.

"Poor Crutchfield," Mrs. Gurney said. We stood in front of Mr. Crutchfield's house. An upstairs light—in the bedroom, I knew—was on, although the lower stories were dark and empty. "And Lucy— God, such grief. They loved each other, Kurt." Mrs. Gurney frowned. "They loved each other. And now?"

Actually, the Crutchfields hadn't loved each other—information I alone was privy to. Lucy's grief, I was sure, had to do with the fact that her husband died in a state of absolute misery, and now she would never be able to change things. In Lucy's mind, he would be forever screwing around, and she would be forever waiting for him to cut it out and come home. After he died, she spread the myth of their reconciliation, and everyone believed it, but I knew it to be a lie. Mr. Crutchfield's sense of failure over the marriage was enormous. He blamed himself, as perhaps he should have. But I remember, one night earlier in the summer, telling him it was O.K., that if he was unhappy with Lucy, it was fine to fuck around. He said, You think so? I said, Sure, go for it.

Of course, you might ask, what did I know? At thirteen, I'd never even smooched with a girl, but I had nothing to lose by encouraging him. He was drunk, he was miserable, and I had a job, and that job was to get him home and try to prevent him from dwelling too much on himself.

It was that night, the night I took Mr. Crutchfield home, as I walked back to our house, that I developed the theory of the black hole, and it helped me immeasurably in conducting this business of steering drunks around the Point. The idea was this—that at a certain age, a black hole emerged in the middle of your life, and everything got sucked into it, and you knew, forever afterward, that it was there, this dense negative space, and yet you went on, you struggled, you made your money, you had some babies, you got wasted, and you pretended it wasn't there and never looked directly at it, if you could manage the trick. I imagined that this black hole existed somewhere just behind you and also somewhere just in front of you, so that you were always leaving it behind and entering it at the same time. I hadn't worked out the spatial thing too carefully, but that's what I imagined. Sometimes the hole was only a pinprick in the mind, often it was vast, frequently it fluctuated, beating like a heart, but it was always there, and when you got drunk, thinking to escape, you only noticed it more. Anyway, when I discovered this, much like an astronomer gazing out at the universe, I thought I had the key— and it became a policy with me never to let one of my drunks think too much and fall backward or forward into the black hole. We're going home, I would say to them—we're just going home.

I wondered how old Mrs. Gurney was, and guessed thirty-seven. I imagined her black hole was about the size of a sewer cap.

MRS. GURNEY SAT DOWN on the hull of an overturned life raft. She reached up under her skirt and pulled her nylons off, rolling them down her legs, tossing the little black doughnuts into the wind. I fetched them, too, and stuffed them into the straps of her sandals.

"Much better," she said.

"We're not far now, Mrs. Gurney. We'll have you home in no time."

She managed to stand up on her own. She floated past me, heading toward the sea. A tangle of ghostly gray driftwood—old tree stumps, logs loosed from booms, planks—barred the way, being too treacherous for her to climb in such a drunken state, I thought, but Mrs. Gurney just kept going, her hair exploding in the wind, her skirt billowing like a sail, her arms wavering like a trapeze artist's high up on the wire.

"Mrs. Gurney?" I called.

"I want—" she started, but the wind tore her words away. Then she sat down on a log, and when I got there, she was holding her head in her hands and vomiting between her legs. Vomit, and the spectacle of adults vomiting, was one of the unpleasant aspects of this job. I hated to see these people in such an abject position. Still, after three years, I knew in which closets the mops and sponges and cleansers were kept in quite a few houses on the Point.

I patted Mrs. Gurney's shoulder and said, "That's O.K., that's O.K., just go right ahead. You'll feel much better when it's all out."

She choked and spat, and a trail of silver hung from her lip down to the sand. "Oh, damn it all, Kurt. Just damn it all to hell." She raised her head. "Look at me, just look at me, will you?"

She looked a little wretched, but all right. I'd seen worse.

"Have a cigarette, Mrs. Gurney," I said. "Calm down."

I didn't smoke, myself—thinking it was a disgusting habit—but I'd observed from past experience that a cigarette must taste good to a person who has just thrown up. A cigarette or two seemed to calm people right down, giving them something simple to concentrate on.

Mrs. Gurney handed me her cigarettes. I shook one from the pack and stuck it in my mouth. I struck half a dozen matches before I got one going, cupping the flame against the wind in the style of old war movies. I puffed the smoke. I passed Mrs. Gurney the cigarette, and she dragged on it, abstracted, gazing off. I waited, and let her smoke in peace.

"I feel god-awful," Mrs. Gurney groaned.

"It'll go away, Mrs. Gurney. You're drunk. We just have to get you home."

"Look at my skirt," she said.

True, she'd messed it up a little, barfing on herself, but it was nothing a little soap and water couldn't fix. I told her that.

"How old am I, Kurt?" she retorted. I pretended to think it over, then aimed low.

"Twenty-nine? Good God!" Mrs. Gurney stared out across the water, at the deep, black shadow of Hat Island, and I looked, too, and it was remarkable, the way that darkness carved itself out of the darkness all around. But I could marvel over this when I was off duty.

"I'm thirty-eight, Kurt," she screamed. "Thirty-eight, thirty-eight, thirty-eight!"

I was losing her. She was heading for ten on a scale of ten.

"On a dark night, bumping around," she said, "you can't tell the difference between thirty-eight and forty. Fifty! Sixty!" She pitched her cigarette in a high, looping arc that exploded against a log in a spray of gold sparks. "Where am I going, God damn it?"

"You're going home, Mrs. Gurney. Hang tough."

"I want to die."

A few boats rocked in the wind, and a seal moaned out on the diving raft, the cries carrying away from us, south, downwind. A red warning beacon flashed out on the sandbar. Mrs. Gurney clambered over the driftwood and weaved across the wet sand toward the sea. She stood by the shoreline, and for a moment I thought she might hurl herself into the breach, but she didn't. She stood on the shore's edge, the white waves swirling at her feet, and dropped her skirt around her ankles. She was wearing a silky white slip underneath, the sheen like a bike reflector in the moonlight. She waded out into the water and squatted down, scrubbing her skirt. Then she walked out of the water and stretched herself on the sand.

"Mrs. Gurney?"

"I've got the fucking spins."

Her eyes were closed. I suggested that she open them. "It makes a difference," I said. "And sit up, Mrs. Gurney. That makes a difference, too."

"You've had the spins?" Mrs. Gurney asked. "Don't tell me you sneak into your mother's liquor cabinet, Kurt Pittman. Don't tell me that. Please, just please spare me that. Jesus Christ, I couldn't take it. Really, I couldn't take it, Kurt. Just shut the fuck up about that, all right?"

I'd never taken a drink in my life. "I don't drink, Mrs. Gurney."

"I don't drink, Mrs. Gurney," she repeated. "You prig."

I wondered what time it was, and how long we'd been gone.

"Do you know how suddenly life can turn?" Mrs. Gurney asked. "How bad it can get?"

At first I didn't say anything. This kind of conversation didn't lead anywhere. Mrs. Gurney was drunk and belligerent. She was looking for an enemy. "We need to get you home, Mrs. Gurney," I said. "That's my only concern."

"Your only concern," Mrs. Gurney said, imitating me again. "Lucky you."

I stood there, slightly behind Mrs. Gurney. I was getting tired, but sitting down in the sand might indicate to her that where we were was O.K., and it wasn't. We needed to get beyond this stage, this tricky stage of groveling in the sand and feeling depressed, and go to sleep.

"We're not getting anywhere like this," I said.

"I've got cottonmouth," Mrs. Gurney said. She made fish movements with her mouth. She was shivering, too. She clasped her knees and tucked her head between her legs, trying to ball herself up like a potato bug.

"Kurt," Mrs. Gurney said, looking up at me, "do you think I'm beautiful?"

I switched the sandals I was holding to the other hand. First I'll tell you what I said, and then I'll tell you what I was thinking. I said yes, and I said it immediately. And why? Because I sensed that questions that didn't receive an immediate response fell away into silence and were never answered. They got sucked into the black hole. I'd observed this, and I knew the trick was to close the gap in Mrs. Gurney's mind, to bridge that spooky silence between the question and the answer. There she was, drunk, sick, shivering, loveless, sitting in the sand and asking me, a mere boy, if I thought she was beautiful. I said yes, because I knew it wouldn't hurt, or cost me anything but one measly breath, though that wasn't really my answer. The answer was in the immediacy, the swiftness of my response, stripped of all uncertainty and hesitation.

"Yes," I said.

MRS. GURNEY LAY DOWN AGAIN in the sand. She unbuttoned her blouse and unfastened her brassiere.

I scanned the dark, and fixed my eyes on a tug hauling a barge north through the Passage, up to the San Juans.

Mrs. Gurney sat up. She shrugged out of her blouse and slipped her bra off and threw them into the wind. Again I fetched her things from where they fell, and held the bundle at my side, waiting.

"That's better," Mrs. Gurney said, arching her back and stretching her hands in the air, waggling them as if she were some kind of dignitary in a parade. "The wind blowing, it's like a spirit washing over you."

"We should go, Mrs. Gurney."

"Sit, Kurt, sit," she said, patting the wet sand. The imprint of her hand remained there a few seconds, then flattened and vanished. The tide was coming in fast, and it would be high tonight, with the moon full.

I crouched down, a few feet away.

"So you think I'm beautiful?" Mrs. Gurney said. She stared ahead, not looking at me, letting the words drift in the wind.

"This really isn't a question of beauty or not beauty, Mrs. Gurney."

"No?"

"No," I said. "I know your husband doesn't love you, Mrs. Gurney. That's the problem here."

"Beauty," she sang.

"No. Like they say, beauty is in the eye of the beholder. You don't have a beholder anymore, Mrs. Gurney."

"The moon and the stars," she said, "the wind and the sea."

Wind, sea, stars, moon: we were in uncharted territory, and it was my fault. I'd let us stray from the goal, and now it was nowhere in sight. I had to steer this thing back on course, or we'd end up talking about God.

"Get dressed, Mrs. Gurney; it's cold. This isn't good. We're going home."

She clasped her knees, and rocked back and forth. She moaned, "It's so far."

"It's not far," I said. "We can see it from here."

"Someday I'm leaving all this to you," Mrs. Gurney said, waving her hands around in circles, pointing at just about everything in the world. "When I get it from my husband, after the divorce, I'm leaving it to you. That's a promise, Kurt. I mean that. It'll be in my will. You'll get a call. You'll get a call and you'll know I'm dead. But you'll be happy, you'll be very happy, because all of this will belong to you."

Her house was only a hundred yards away. A wind sock, full of the air that passed through it, whipped back and forth on a tall white pole. Her two kids had been staying in town most of that summer. I wasn't sure if they were up this weekend. She'd left the porch light on for herself.

"You'd like all this, right?" Mrs. Gurney asked.

"Now is not the time to discuss it," I said.

Mrs. Gurney lay back down in the sand. "The stars have tails," she said. "When they spin."

I looked up; they seemed fixed in place to me.

"The first time I fell in love I was fourteen. I fell in love when I was fifteen, I fell in love when I was sixteen, seventeen, eighteen. I just kept falling, over and over," Mrs. Gurney said. "This eventually led to marriage." She packed a lump of wet sand on her chest. "It's so stupid—you know where I met him?"

I assumed she was referring to Jack, to Mr. Gurney. "No," I said.

"On a golf course, can you believe it?"

"Do you golf, Mrs. Gurney?"

"No! Hell no."

"Does Jack?"

"No."

I couldn't help her—it's the stories that don't make sense that drunks like to repeat. From some people, I'd been hearing the same stories every summer for the last three years—the kind everyone thinks is special, never realizing how everyone tells pretty much the same one, never realizing how all those stories blend, one to the next, and bleed into each other.

"I'm thirsty," Mrs. Gurney said. "I'm so homesick."

"We're close now," I said.

"That's not what I mean," she said. "You don't know what I mean."

"Maybe not," I said. "Please put your shirt on, Mrs. Gurney."

"I'll kill myself," Mrs. Gurney said. "I'll go home and I'll kill myself."

"That won't get you anywhere."

"I'll show them."

"You'd just be dead, Mrs. Gurney. Then you'd be forgotten."

"Crutchfield isn't forgotten. Poor Crutchfield. The flag's at half-mast."

"This year," I said. "Next year it'll be back where it always is."

"My boys wouldn't forget."

That was certainly true, I thought, but I didn't want to get into it.

Mrs. Gurney sat up. She shook her head back and forth, wildly, and sand flew from it. Then she stood, wobbling. I held the shirt out to her, looking down. She wiggled her toes, burrowing them into the sand.

"Look at me," Mrs. Gurney said.

"I'd rather not, Mrs. Gurney," I said. "Tomorrow you'll be glad I didn't."

For a moment we didn't speak, and into that empty space rushed the wind, the waves, the moaning seal out on the diving raft. I looked up, into Mrs. Gurney's eyes, which were dark green and floating in tears. She stared back, but kind of vaguely, and I wondered what she saw.

I had the feeling that the first to flinch would lose.

She took the shirt from my hand.

I looked.

In this I had no experience, but I knew what I saw was not young flesh. Her breasts sagged away like sacks of wet sand, slumping off to either side. They were quite enormous, I thought, although I had nothing to compare them with. There were long whitish scars on them, as if a wild man or a bear had clawed her. The nipples were purple in the moonlight, and they puckered in the cold wind. The gold, squiggling loops of chain shone against the dark of her neck, and the V of her tan line made everything else seem astonishingly white. The tan skin of her chest looked like parchment, like the yellowed, crinkled page of some ancient text, maybe the Bible, or the Constitution, the original copy, or even the rough draft.

Mrs. Gurney slipped the shirt over her shoulders and let it flap there in the wind. It blew off and tumbled down the beach. She sighed. Then she stepped closer and leaned toward me. I could smell her—the pepper, the bananas.

"Mrs. Gurney," I said, "let's go home now." The tide was high enough for us to feel the first foamy white reaches of the waves wash around our feet. The receding waves dragged her shirt into the sea, and then the incoming waves flung it back. It hung there in the margin, agitated. We were looking into each other's eyes. Up so close, there was nothing familiar in hers; they were just glassy and dark and expressionless.

It was then, I was sure, that her hand brushed the front of my trunks. I don't remember too much of what I was thinking, if I was, and this, this not thinking too clearly, might have been my downfall. What is it out there that indicates the right way? I might have gone down all the way. I might have sunk right there. I knew all the words for it, and they were all short and brutal. Fuck, poke, screw. A voice told me I could get away with it. Who will know the difference, the voice asked. It said, Go for it. And I knew the voice, knew it was the same voice that told Mr. Crutchfield to go ahead, fuck around. We were alone—nothing out there but the moon and the sea. I looked at Mrs. Gurney, looked into her eyes, and saw two black lines pouring out of them and running in crazy patterns down her cheeks.

I felt I should be gallant, or tender, and kiss Mrs. Gurney. I felt I should say something, then I felt I should be quiet. It seemed as if the moment were poised, as if everything were fragile, and held together with silence.

We moved up the beach, away from the shore and the incoming tide, and the sand beneath the surface still held some of the day's warmth.

I took off my T-shirt. "Put this on," I said.

She tugged it on, inside out, and I gathered up her sandals and stockings and her bra. We kept silent. We worked our way over the sand, over the tangle of driftwood, the wind heaving at us from the north.

We crossed the boardwalk, and I held Mrs. Gurney's elbow as we went up the steps of her house. Inside, I found the aspirin and poured a glass of apple cider, and brought these to her in bed, where she'd already curled up beneath a heavy Mexican blanket. She looked like she was sleeping underneath a rug. "I'm thirsty," she said, and drank down the aspirin with the juice. A lamp was on. Mrs. Gurney's silver hair splayed out against the pillow, poking like bike spokes, every which way. I knelt beside the bed, and she touched my hand and parted her lips to speak, but I squeezed her hand and her eyes closed. Soon she was asleep.

As I was going downstairs, her two boys, Mark and Timmy, came out of their bedroom and stared at me from the landing.

"Mommy home?" asked Timmy, who was three.

"Yeah," I said. "She's in bed, she's sleeping."

They stood there on the lighted landing, blinking and rubbing knuckles in their eyes, and I stood below them on the steps in the dark.

"Where's the sitter?" I asked.

"She fell asleep," Timmy said.

"You guys should be asleep, too."

"I can't sleep," Timmy said. "Tell a bedtime story."

"I don't know any bedtime stories," I said.

BACK HOME, inside our house, the bright light and smoke stung my eyes. The living room was crowded, but I knew everybody—the Potters, the Shanks, the Capstands, etc. It was noisy and shrill, and someone had cranked up the Victrola, and one of my grandfather's old records was sending a sea of hissing static through the room. I could see on the mantel, through the curling smoke, the shrine Mother had made for Father: his Silver Star and Purple Heart, which he got in Lao Bao, up near Khe Sanh, near the DMZ when he was a medic. His diploma from medical school angled cockeyed off a cut nail. A foul ball he'd caught at a baseball game, his reading glasses, a pocketknife, a stethoscope, a framed Hippocratic oath with snakes wreathed around what looked like a barber pole. I saw Mother flit through the kitchen with a silver cocktail shaker, jerking it like a percussion instrument. She just kept pacing like a caged animal, rattling cracked ice in the shaker. I couldn't hear any distinct voices above the party noise. I stood there awhile. No one seemed to notice me until Fred, three sheets to the wind, as they say, hoisted his empty glass in the air and said, "Hey, Captain!"

I went into the kitchen. Mother set down the shaker and looked at me. I gave her a hug. "I'm back," I said.

Then I crossed into my room and stripped the sheets from my bed. I hung them out the window and shook the sand away. I tossed the sheets back on the bed and stretched out, but I couldn't get to sleep. I got up and pulled one of Father's old letters out from under my mattress. I went out the back door. It was one of those nights on the Point when the blowing wind, the waves breaking in crushed white lines against the shore, the grinding sand, the moon-washed silhouettes of the huddled houses, the slapping of buoys offshore—when all of this seems to have been going on for a long, long time, and you feel eternity looking down on you. I sat on the swing. The letter was torn at the creases, and I opened it carefully, tilting it into the moonlight. It was dated 1966, and written to Mother. The print was smudged and hard to see.

First, the old news: thank you for the necktie. I'm not sure when I'll get a chance to wear it, but thanks. Now for my news. I've been wounded, but don't worry. I'm O.K.

For several days a company had been deployed on the perimeter of this village—the rumor was that somehow the fields had been planted with VC mines. The men work with tanks—picture tanks moving back and forth over a field like huge lawnmowers. They clear the way by exploding the mines. Generally VC mines are antipersonnel, and the idea is that the tanks are supposed to set off the mines and absorb the explosions. Tanks can easily sustain the blows, and the men inside are safe. A textbook operation. Simple. Yesterday they set off twelve mines. Who knows how they got there?

Clearing the perimeter took several days. Last night they thought they were done. But as the men were jumping off the tanks, one of them landed right on a mine. I was the first medic to reach him. His feet and legs were blown off, blown away up to his groin. I've never seen anything so terrible, but here's what I remember most clearly: a piece of shrapnel had penetrated his can of shaving cream, and it was shooting a stream of white foam about five feet in the air. Blood spilling everywhere, and then this fountain of white arcing out of his back. The pressure inside the can kept hissing. The kid was maybe nineteen. "Doc, I'm a mess," he said. I called in a medevac. I started packing dressings, then saw his eyes lock up, and tried to revive him with heart massage. The kid died before the shaving cream was done spraying.

Everything became weirdly quiet, considering the havoc, and then suddenly the LZ got hot and we took fire—fifteen minutes of artillery and incoming mortar fire, then quiet again. Nothing, absolutely nothing. I took a piece of shrapnel in my back, but don't worry. I'm all right, though I won't have occasion to wear that tie soon. I didn't even know I was wounded until I felt the blood, and even then I thought it was someone else's.

Strange, during that fifteen minutes of action I felt no fear. But there's usually not much contact with the enemy. Often you don't see a single VC the whole time. Days pass without any contact. They're out there, you know, yet you never see them. Just mines, booby traps. I'm only a medic, and my contact with the enemy is rarely direct—what I see are the wounded men and the dead, the bodies. I see the destruction, and I have begun to both fear and hate the Vietnamese—even here in South Vietnam, I can't tell whose side they're on. Every day I visit a nearby village and help a local doctor vaccinate children. The morning after the attack I felt the people in the village were laughing at me because they knew an American had died. Yesterday I returned to the same village. Everything quiet, business as usual, but I stood there, surrounded by hooches, thinking of that dead kid, and for a moment I felt the urge to even the score somehow.

What am I saying, sweetie? I'm a medic, trained to save lives. Every day I'm closer to death than most people ever get, except in their final second on earth. It's a world of hurt—that's the phrase we use—and things happen over here, things you just can't keep to yourself. I've seen what happens to men who try. They're consumed by what they've seen and done, they grow obsessive, and slowly they lose sight of the job they're supposed to be doing. I have no hard proof of this, but I think in this condition men open themselves up to attack. You've got to talk things out, get everything very clear in your mind. Lucky for me I've got a buddy over here who's been under fire too, and can understand what I'm feeling. That helps.

I'm sorry to write like this, but in your letter you said you wanted to know everything. It's not in my power to say what this war means to you or anyone back home, but I can describe what happens, and if you want, I'll continue doing that. For me, at least, it's a comfort to know someone's out there, far away, who can't really understand, and I hope is never able to. I'll write again soon.

All love,

Henry

I'D SNAGGED THIS LETTER from a box Mother kept in her room, under the bed. There were other kinds of letters in the box, letters about love and family and work, but I didn't think Mother would miss this one, which was just about war. Father never talked much about his tours in Vietnam, but he would if I asked. Out of respect, I learned not to ask too much, but I knew about Zippo raids, trip flares, bouncing bettys, hand frags, satchel charges, and such, and when he was angry, or sad, Father often peppered his speech with slang he'd picked up, like *titi*, which means "little," and *didi mow*, which means "go quickly," and *xin loi*, meaning "sorry about that."

I tucked the letter away. I got the swing going real good, and I rose up, then fell, rose and fell, seeing, then not seeing. When the swing was going high enough I let go and sailed through the open air, landing in an explosion of soft sand. I wiped the grains out of my eyes. My eyes watered, and everything was unclear. Things toppled and blew in the wind. A striped beach umbrella rolled across the playfield, twirling like a pinwheel. A sheet from someone's clothesline flapped loose and sailed away. I thought of my nightmare, of Father's balloon tied to a stringbean. I looked up at the sky, and it was black, with some light. There were stars, millions of them like tiny holes in something, and the moon, like a bigger hole in the same thing. White holes. I thought of Mrs. Gurney and her blank eyes and the black pouring out of them. Was it the wind, a sudden gust kicking up and brushing my trunks? It happened so quickly. Had she tried to touch me? Had she? I stretched out in the sand. The wind gave me goose bumps. Shivering, I listened. From inside the house, I heard the men laughing, the ice clinking, the women shrieking. Everything in there was still hysterical. I'd never get to sleep. I decided to stay awake. They would all be going home, but until then I'd wait outside.

I lay there, very quietly. I brushed some sand off me. I waited.

It was me who found Father, that morning. I'd gone up to get some creosote out of the trunk of his car. It was a cold, gray, misty morning, the usual kind we have, and in the grass field above the parking lot there was a family of deer, chewing away, looking around, all innocent. And there he was, sitting in the car. I opened the passenger door. At first my eyes kind of separated from my brain, and I saw everything real slow, like you might see a movie, or something far away that wasn't happening to you. Some of his face was gone. One of his eyes was staring out. He was still breathing, but his lungs worked like he'd swallowed a yard of chunk gravel or sand. He was twitching. I touched his hand and the fingers curled around mine, gripping, but it was just nerves, an old reaction or something, because he was brain-dead already. My imagination jumped right out of its box when he grabbed me. I knew right away I was being grabbed by a dead man. I got away. I ran away. In our house I tried to speak, but there were no words. I started pounding the walls and kicking over the furniture and breaking stuff. I couldn't see, I heard falling. I ran around the house holding and ripping at my head. Eventually Mother caught me. I just pointed up to the car. You understand, I miss Father, miss having him around to tell me what's right and what's wrong, or to talk about *boom-boom*, which is sex, or just to go salmon fishing out by Hat Island and not worry about things, either way, but I also have to say, never again do I want to see anything like what I saw that morning. I never, as long as I live, want to find another dead person. He wasn't even a person then, just a blown-up thing, just crushed-up garbage. Part of his head was blasted away, and there was blood and hair and bone splattered on the windshield. It looked like he'd just driven the car through something awful, like he needed to use the windshield wipers, needed to switch the blades on high and clear the way, except that the wipers wouldn't do him any good, because the mess was all on the inside.

Robert Hass

On the Coast near Sausalito

1

I won't say much for the sea
except that it was, almost,
the color of sour milk.
The sun in that clear
unmenacing sky was low,
angled off the grey fissure of the cliffs,
hills dark green with manzanita.

Low tide: slimed rocks
mottled brown and thick with kelp
like the huge backs of ancient tortoises
merged with the grey stone
of the breakwater, sliding off
to antediluvian depths.
The old story: here filthy life begins.

2

Fish-
ing, as Melville said,
"to purge the spleen,"
to put to task my clumsy hands
my hands that bruise by
not touching
pluck the legs from a prawn,
peel the shell off,
and curl the body twice about a hook.

3

The cabezone is not highly regarded
by fishermen, except Italians
who have the grace
to fry the pale, almost bluish flesh
in olive oil with a sprig
of fresh rosemary.

The cabezone, an ugly atavistic fish,
as old as the coastal shelf
it feeds upon
has fins of duck's-web thickness,
resembles a prehistoric toad,
and is delicately sweet.

Catching one, the fierce quiver of surprise
and the line's tension
are a recognition.

4

But it's strange to kill
for the sudden feel of life.
The danger is
to moralize
that strangeness.
Holding the spiny monster in my hands
his bulging purple eyes
were eyes and the sun was
almost tangent to the planet
on our uneasy coast.
Creature and creature,
we stared down centuries.

Maria Flook

Diving Alone

Every night she ropes the ship
to her legs.
In the lead hull of memory
blind creatures find a home.

Why do they say "drift to sleep"?
Truth could be salt,
it stings her mouth
and dissolves while she is speaking.
Faith is the raft she builds
that, without her, glides away.

At night she makes preparations.
Heavy clothing is removed,
the heart becomes strict with the lungs.
Holding a deep breath keeps his ghost
like a hard body inside, helps sink her.

She learned to swim early
on the flat palms of her father.
Pelvis and breastbone, wet fingertips.
She learned to swallow without thirst,
breathe without foundation.

Why do they say "deep sleep"?
Night is a still surface
and she is beneath it.

If life is a voyage, she'll go back
and forth for violets.
If love is an anchor, she will use
his slender knife and set herself free.
If death is black water
she will see through it.

The Pier

When I reached the harbor
the tour boats were sailing
out, others returning.
From a great distance,
people waved their arms
to whom, to what friends—
perhaps they saw the shore;
the shore is dear to all.
I like the way a pier ends
abruptly, madly, in the deep.
But here, useful ropes
are wasted as decorations,
the colored nets and floats
like discarded party favors.
I turn my back and rest
my full weight against the flat top
of the blackest piling.
The water's broken surface,
a looking glass that parts
the face from the body.
Strangers see I'm unhappy
and edge away, nearer
the concessions' bright awnings.

Is the sea jealous of the sky
or does the sky seek pleasure
in these twisting sheets?
White birds are mirrored,
or do gulls mimic
the rough wings of the surf?
I fell for it all,
two deceptions, the tides—
one that pressed close
its soapy veils, washing my name
from hers, and one that pulled back
leaving all creatures fluttering,
the squid's black word exposed.

Kristina McGrath

In the Quiet

The colors of their tiny coats glittered at first sight, then dulled to plain cotton hauled with its creases from drawers, flattened by suitcases, wrinkled by buses—but Helen, Eddy, and Lulie Hallissey caught in sunlight were glorious, she thought, and the new of pink yellow red, so long as it lasted at the corner of her blue eye. It was nothing really. It was summer glare. It was only a moment that cast light on their faces.

Anna Hallissey was on her own for the very first time in Erie, Pennsylvania, on a two-day trip to the lake; it was for their sake. The colors of their coats, the pressed blue sky of August, wide without a wrinkle over gray-brown water, made her heart fall backward, like a rare somersault, as she blinked in the corners of sunlight, in love with what was here and capable of leaving.

Their shy pink feet stepped from sandy curbs. Hesitant, skipping, looking both ways, they were stumbling into her toes, she was hugging their wrists. Listen, she told them. That rush of water in the silence. It was only for an instant.

Far below her on either side, one held to her skirt, the other to her hand; the oldest she had by the wrist in front of her and then let go.

The oldest snapped her hand away all the while they walked. But she had managed it. They were safely across the street. And in the stillness of the other side, she could guess what they would have for supper.

She could see them (laughing, with their hot dogs and bright yellow mustard) to the smallest detail, sitting in their circle of three around the oilcloth-covered table checked with blue and white squares darkened at the edges, while she hovered above them, wiping her hands on a towel, and it grieved her in a funny sort of way, how life went on, even on vacation in Erie, the four of them in a too-small room, eating supper.

But she would amuse them. She would make this a happy day. After supper she would set them on her ankle one by one, on a little white horsey for a ridee ridee to town. They were too old for it, she knew it. God knows, even the youngest had to get herself to and from kindergarten this last year. (I'm sorry, it's necessary, you're a big girl, she told her, skimming her hand, apologizing for it.) And Lulie Hallissey went off each morning, a windblown thing, down Dorothy Avenue, looking back all the way to the very last second of the corner, while from the porch she shooed her forward with her hand, urging it into her, the will to do it.

They were good children. They did what they were told to do, and she wanted something nice, something once in a blue moon, to give them. They lay curved on carpets for hours at a time in their deep habit of quiet. Their tongues found their way to the bottom of their lips. They made valentines from paper doilies, infinite numbers of them, and always for her, way past February. I love you Mummy, they always told her that. More than anythink in the hole wirld. They snipped at magazine pictures. They colored like mad. But today and tomorrow, she was determined to give them two full days of sunlight in open air.

They would surprise her. Struck by sunlight from their quiet, they would be lifted, cured, and giggling, they would dive upward, burst forward, be quick from their chairs, recovered, at the sight of water.

She would follow their lead. She would raise her chin, and by the compass of their willingness she would traipse, hating the sunlight and even the thought of water, but loving the colors that light and the lake made of their skin and thin straight hair. She would be careful to count the stop signs, study the bungalows along the way, an orange flowerpot on a kitchen sill, for the way back. Otherwise, unused to travel, her sense of direction would vanish like a bubble. Then what would she do? The thought of her voice asking for help in this strange land made her determined to find her own way.

She stopped. (The oldest was doing it again, she was pulling away.) She stood by a row of one-story clapboard houses. Painted white, they all looked the same and it made her dizzy. (Quit that, you stay close to me, Helen, she told her and slapped her hand.) She made them wait and hold to her skirt, then the boy ran ahead like crazy. Running ahead like crazy, saying Hey, Watch me, why don't you? Anna's eyes were blue, ice blue and searching into the distance. (Eddy, you come back here right this minute.) Then he popped up like toast right by her side.

Tiny bungalows, she thought, disappointed. Slightly ramshackle and all the same by the brown water. But Anna Hallissey had a better, bluer plan for water. She had cathedrals while the world had bungalows.

The houses were set close to the broad street, with small screened-in porches tucked back at their sides, their steps speckled brown with sand. Beyond the houses, in the smallness between them, the open space of the lake was new to her. It caught her eye, pulling her out, into itself, where she didn't want to go. She would catch her breath. She would sit on the beach and go over it in her head, clapboard by clapboard, bungalow by bungalow, flowerpot by sill.

They had made it this far. She was managing and allowed herself to look at the sky again. She stood there, her feet planted firm like a tree, with her hand on her hip, with her chin upraised. And there it was, only for an instant, pure beauty.

These years it had rarely happened to her that the sky, a color, a tree she met in life was larger, brighter, better, more blue or bent into green than what she knew with shut eyes. As far back as she could remember, winding her way through the streets of Pittsburgh where there was always something to adore, she would laugh at the lazy sound of her own petticoat—she would; and she was thrilled: a certain afternoon sky, stray dog or sleeping cat, a new set of streets on the mill side of town, the colors of steel mills flaring up between rivers and railtrack in rain, and returning home, a strange plum color her furniture cast in shadow; and she was thrilled.

But now a sadness always set in. She was walking along the course of an afternoon or these years, still capable of surprise, of joy even, like a low green water ebbing within her, and after the beauty of a mongrel, the pout of its face, after the deep gray thrill of Sacred Heart Church in Shadyside with its ribs of stone, its reach, there was a sadness, it was heavy on her eyelids, and she was no longer changed by the sky or a plum shadow. Beauty couldn't do that anymore, and she knew it. Nothing changed you the way sorrow or catastrophe did. And nothing was better than what she found in the darkness of her own shut eyes in the few moments she stole from pure air.

She patted their little rear ends, Let's go, she said, This is our lucky day, and they trudged forward. After something glorious, it was the same world, she thought to herself, and she was the same woman, her husband the same man. (She had left him sitting in his chair over a year ago, and he was weeping, but it was still the same. He was still her husband.)

She half expected to see him, poking out from behind a telephone pole or diving upward, a terrible surprise, from the middle of Lake Erie. (He did it all the time. He followed her. He would find her, he would take her to court he said, he would bring the priests.) But she knew what she would say this time. *Somebody,* she would tell him (he was swimming toward her now in the smallness between the houses), was going to get taken to court if this doesn't stop right now. She would settle it once and for all.

Race, she almost said to them, lifting her hand, ready to shoo them down the block. But she would let them amble. They liked to kick the stones, they liked to swing their arms through air, they liked to skip then dawdle. She let them.

She was always pulling them along the streets of Pittsburgh, hurrying their feet on the way back home from the supermarket. She would get them on their toes, clatter her little teacup feet and tell them, Like this, Run like the dickens. She would tell them a lie, say it was a race. Let's race, she would tell them whenever she saw the turquoise of his Chevy, the white shirt, the hunch of his shoulders against the steering wheel as he waited outside the Giant Eagle Supermarket on Highland Avenue, beating out a rhythm on the dashboard, singing (he actually had the nerve to sing). She cut across Highland on the diagonal in the middle of the block and all the while down the long stretch of Elwood Street his car crept behind them, with the radio turned low. On cat paws, insistent, he would not let go; and she shooed them forward, like butterflies, she thought, in their colored jackets. With her arms wrapped tight around brown paper bags toppling with cans, her hands waved them on at intersections, searching from under bags of groceries for their heads bumped this way and that. Their hands fluttered like eyelids. She jingled her keys to make them hurry. Get inside, she told them. When the fat brass lock tumbled into place on Dorothy Avenue, she breathed.

But they were slow as molasses now, and they poured themselves sweet down the bright streets of Erie. One time, she remembered it now, she pulled the drapes and herded them into bed in daylight. She picked them up (they were too old for it) and lay them down. I don't care what time it is; we're going to bed. But like a bat out of hell and with an Oh My God, we forgot our prayers (a prayer of thanks for another happy day, she had thought at the time and laughed, she really did laugh), she jumped from her bed, she gathered them up, she held their hands, In the Name of the Father, the Son, and listened while they prayed. With an eye on the door, Mea culpa, she thought, she would sit in empty churches, she would kiss Mary on her beige china lips, she would eat priest bread.

Sunday mass was a terrible thing. And as she walked along the streets of Erie the far-away smell of incense, the underwater smell of churches, made her head reel. He had moved to their part of Pittsburgh. He had joined their church. All of a sudden there he was one Sunday at the 10 o'clock. She caught the corner of his shiny blue suit behind the stone pillar speckled with silver. And Holy Mary, Mother of God, she had said at the time, he was coming around with the collection basket of all things, her children were dropping their little green envelopes of quarters into his basket, and all she could think of was his brand-new turquoise '56 Chevy, and child support payments, how he never managed to make them. She lowered her head. She put her arms around her children's shoulders, she jumbled them up.

He was gone now. He was behind her now. It was August in the streets of Erie and she was on her own. As they crossed the street to the beach, she put her arms around her children's shoulders. She lowered her head to hug them, she jumbled them up inside her arms, snapping the white pearl from her ear, and her youngest (with an eye held close to her cheek) saw it, the lobe bright pink like a punishment.

The priests had come and gone. She stepped up onto the curb and blessed relief, she said to herself, because she was rid of the earrings and didn't know what she was thinking of, wearing them to the beach in the first place. Priests, she said, hopefully she had put an end to that, too.

He had brought them to the house on Dorothy Avenue twice already. Married forever in the eye of God, they wanted her to know that, and she knew it was true. You're living in a state of sin, Father Rawley was certain of it. I have no thoughts of ever marrying again, she told him. Mrs., said Father Rawley. He would consider excommunication if she didn't go back. Your place is with him, he told her, He's a good man.

She remembered she breathed then a single breath. She took it from the air around her, it was blowing in from the yard where her children played, where she had sent them (Get outside, your daddy and his priests need to see me again), where they sat cross-legged in a circle, tribal and decided with fistfuls of earth, where they made priests into grass and brushed them from their clothes, where they loved her more than God. She took one good breath. I'm sorry, Father, but you're not a mother. She asked them to leave. She bowed her head and thanked them. Thank you, Fathers, but you're not mothers.

At the side of her eye she could see him slouched on her green sofa, with his legs flung open, pretending he belonged there. Look, she told him, These are the rules when you want to see the kids. He was reading the bottom of her knickknacks. He was spitting into his handkerchief. My husband, she thought. Even if she never saw him again (which she preferred), even if he never again roared up to the curb to visit her children. But they were his children, too. And she told them so. He's still your father, no matter what he does or doesn't do.

Either the world was ultimately small and disappointing, she decided, or her dreams were impossibly large and out of place. (She dreamed a cathedral, she dreamed a woods, blue lake; he would never find her there.) Either her dreams were just plain silly or learned of God and the stuff of angels. What could be better in a time of need than this cathedral looming at the tip of her nose, this deep woods nestled in the palm of her hand? Nothing, she thought. Except for love, she said, of her three.

This was more than she could imagine. At times she did not feel capable of its immensity but preferred to settle on a stitch, a sandwich, a blanket, a sweater, a plum. Their small needs saved her from that precipice where she loved them, or where she loved her father, or her husband once, above all things. Her husband needed a strong cup of coffee with five sugars. Her father needed a weak cup of tea, mixed with four sugars and Carnation evaporated milk. She would pour the tea for her father, she would pour the coffee, she would save herself.

Even as a girl (before they met, before she fell in love) she understood, from her third-floor window over Manon's Drugstore, how space extended, how worlds unraveled into worlds, and in the middle of it all, there was something glorious: the comfort of her own face. She saw it swimming there in black window glass. The sky was just too large, and love, she thought, it was all a whirl; it caught her eye, it tugged at her sleeves, pulling her out, into itself, where she didn't want to go. But she did, she went. And, she could feel herself walking, floating really, above her smallness in a cotton dress, alone on a road too wide and long and too silent to mention more than once or twice in this life.

But with three kids now and on her own, there just wasn't time for the sky, and it suited her fine, it saved her. She took in ironing, she washed her neighbor's floors. But she did promise herself a few things. One, she would make a cake for her kids every two weeks, it was important. Two, she would raise them to be good people. Three, she would make herself go bowling every Tuesday night, she would buy new shoes and force herself. And four, she would get them across the street.

They were not quite there but the sound of water was larger now and they did, they quickened their step. Growing lighter from their toes upward, they would, they would be happy. But then she thought of supper again and she knew it was true, her oldest did not like hot dogs. She could see it now, she would have to walk from place to place, reading menus out loud until they agreed. Helen should have whatever she liked. And in the long search for supper, for something that would please all three, the familiars of home had come to Erie, to this strange land.

Even on this vacation, the first and probably the last, there was the nagging plainness of home, in the calls to supper, in the lugging of things, in cans of soup and changes of clothes, in thoughts of great sorrow or marriage. And there, on their way to the beach, at the top of the road, a church wedding of all things, in Erie. People actually married in Erie. They didn't come here just to die in the sun but to marry.

She felt a sadness for the women young and old in their once-a-year hats, for the grandmothers in their girdles, the men stuffed in their navy blue suits in August, the children stiff and poking from their clothes, for the hot imagined room cramfull of someone's distant cousins coming out of the woodwork, lingering at the heavy buffet, and she felt a sorrow because of the spoons, too small and squat, lost in their dishes. At the sight of a church wedding, she imagined the thin little man and the tidy laced bride, their life filled with Sunday visits to a sister's place, filled with birthdays and funerals and washed-down walls, their life in a quiet neighborhood of good people quick to casserole dishes; it insinuated itself, it rose up, and for a moment, her whole family, all her duntes, her cousins, her sister's kids, and all the neighbors with their eyes out for her children, had come to Erie for a polka wedding. She hated weddings.

This tired body was everywhere, she thought, lugging the suitcase filled with God knows what, like coats in August they didn't need. But she wasn't going to let that bother her. In the back of her mind was the plain singular comfort of one's own bed in a rut far away, the dust and travail of home, the oiled rim of her father's brown hat where he tossed it always upside down on the kitchen table, her children's white spreads, their overstuffed beds, or her own thin narrow one, pulled from an upholstered chair. Her bed was a little out of place, neither here nor there, jutting out on the catty-corner in her daughters' room, but the sun came to wake her there and it was hers, one glorious thing.

They made it to the beach. A single cloud rolled overhead, then another. She stepped onto dry sand, her feet sank down, her shoes filled with it. But why did she know these things, she wondered: the miracle of bed, a shaft of sunlight at its foot, how beautiful a hat could be? Where did they come from, this woods or cathedral, this shaft of sunlight from infinite space? Someone had given them to her, she was sure of it.

She stepped across the beach, and decided: she was the one who knew. And she was the servant of her own creations, she owed them something, a story, a word here and there, and no matter what to never lose it, this joy of closing her eyes, of taking the day, the endless flat of the lake, a teacup, a frayed cuff, into the quiet.

They made it to the lake and she could feel the wind too cool on the backs of her children. They spread pink towels midway between the water and the streets of Erie. She sat on her ankles. She looked at the sky. She gave each cloud the evil eye, banishing each one to a small high place. She was determined to give her children two full days of sunlight. Kneeling on the beach she would take her time with the sky. She would listen for any hint of rain, her ear pressed against the hard side of heaven. (And there was a hard side, she had always known that, she just preferred not to admit it.) She would will the sky to be gorgeous, a hot bright weather for her three. Rain would throw them to the wolves, to their small room, and she would not let it happen.

One cloud, like one sadness, was a domino, toppling down all the others. But she would be a landscape with lake, a narrow strip of land, ax-shaped and sunlit, where they would live protected against truthful strangers bearing bad news, where she too would live protected, in the pure culture, the shelter, of herself.

With a sense of beauty that was almost tyranny, Here comes Mr. Sunshine, she said. She insisted on it. And they knew it wasn't true. They could feel it in their sleeves, close to their skin, a chilled sky, the wind tipping up the hairs on their arms. But she was born to testify to the travels of light, the way it rises, abides on windowsills, the way it falls into a room, the flourish there far away on her nice clean woodwork, she could see it in her mind, that shadow of the window cast on her bed, and she was happy.

She was happy because of the way light fell on some poor thing, on some fortunate spot in their new place, apartment number 1 on Dorothy Avenue, or simply for the lack of something terrible like a cracked basin. They had four whole rooms, a whitewashed cellar, and a big green yard. The house gave her confidence with its wide front porch, its three gray pillars. She sat there on the beach and remembered it. She placed it right there at the water's edge in her mind and remembered the first time she saw it.

They drove from one neighborhood to another, from Wilkinsburg to Shadyside in her brother-in-law's Oldsmobile, from a narrow red alley to a tree-lined avenue. He was in real estate and he had found it for them. Good rent was all he told her, two bedrooms, and a big yard for the kids. Her children were all pinched down in the backseat, with bent elbows and crumpled knees, with ankles fallen into shopping bags, packed in with every last inch of what belonged to her now, with everything she took: their clothes, her duntes' blue vases, her books, a little red wagon, and them. They were all pinched down. She could feel them there in between her fingers, little warm pinches of dry brown sand, little salty buds, her babies. But at first sight of 713 Dorothy Avenue, its steep slope of front yard grass, its set of steps with curves of cement on either side, she could feel a commotion behind her head, and they rose up, they fell open, born, hers. Green and hillbound, they swooped down the grass. $100 a month, her brother-in-law told her and she nearly hit the roof. It was just too beautiful for them, she thought for an instant, how could they pay? But it was theirs, she knew it. They must be beautiful, too. She would manage it, and her dad would help; he'd come along.

The gray house on Dorothy Avenue between Elwood Street and Rosary Way towered over front yard grass. It was huge, it was grand,

and it sprang for them from the side of her head, where their eyes had settled on her wavy hair, where the grass edged in, bursting into its hills by her right ear. They were all squinched down; they sprang forward. And what they felt, they knew it was a kind of grace, their very first touch of it. It was a wild feathery thing from their feet upward, from the sky downward, and they were chosen by this flourish in the air, this commotion at the side of her head, that made this hill, this house appear.

Their lives would begin where this house stood. She decided right then and there. For every week that passed, she would let them know, All my children are special. We are all special people around here. We're doing fine.

And so she was determined for their sake, nearly every day of her life, to fall in love with something plain that was set upon a table (a bowl of yellow flowers, a sack of sugar, a stack of white linens). And though it was a sorry thing (plastic flowers, a sad sack, a stack of used linens), her mind embraced it, whatever it was, it was hers, she had bought it with her own money, she had touched it, cleaned it, put it where it belonged, and she would not cast it away. Not a single thing would be lost to her, but it would shine, peculiar, hers, one of a kind, it would live up to her expectations, and she would be happy.

But they knew it wasn't true. (The flowers were faded, the linens worn thin, the sugar damp and clodded. And they were a bother, they could feel the downturn of their lips, pouty and particular. They were hungry, they were cold, they were hot and insistent. They tore their clothes, they refused to wash their hair, and she was bereft of something, out there in the distance, that they could not see.) They knew it from somewhere, in the way her eyelids fluttered down and shut, in the quick butterfly of her hands over their backs, in her tiny breaths hurried like the cat's heartbeat, from her very own bones, the back that stiffened at the sink.

Sometimes she stood at the sink and watched them playing in the yard. She sat on the beach; she stood at the sink. She watched them at their constant play: in motion, forgetful and stained with grass, or mute and concentrated on baseball, with brown tousled hair, bent shoes, naked knees, their shirts coming loose at the waist. And she saw, as in the momentary passing of a cloud, who they were for an instant only in her mind, where they stood quite still in a row, all bundled up in dark winter coats, with a trace of snow on their shoulders. She saw them through some accident of light that made them appear (they had his face) as the makers of her sorrow, the bearers of it, with nothing ahead of them, nothing else they could be. She caught sight of them in some far-off place, their eyelids shut against the wind, their hands and cheeks exposed. And there it was, her loss, it was speckling their shoulders, shutting their eyes.

At times when she watched them play, their joy seemed like such a noisy rambling out-of-order thing, a dangerous intrigue, and she wanted to make them hush. Don't you come in the house with that. Don't you Hi Mum me. Don't you step on my portulaca. You know you just can't go around breaking glass. What made you go and try a stunt like that? You'll rile up the Natalis' dog. Not in the house, you don't. And don't you start with me.

As she watched them play, she remembered herself in a red dress at twenty-one. Fire-engine red. Busty and beautiful, he said too out loud and wagging his head, and the visiting duntes were shocked. She was slipping out the back door over Manon's Drugstore, slipping past her chores, and she didn't care a fig; she was racing down the stairwell, flying out the door. He was behind the wheel, the bend of him, his length, his foot on the gas. Joy was a dangerous thing. It made her slip out the door again and by the time she came back in, she had three children and she was alone.

She sat on the beach, clutching her purse, tucking her skirt down over her knees. She was sitting right beside them but they could see her far off from them and on her own. They were not enough to keep her here, they knew it. But then it did, the sun came out, just as she said it would. And they saw it was true. The clean linens stacked tight, bright sugar, the odd china pieces, cracked, but seamed with glue. Her idea of flowers on the painted sills. The squeaking of laundry lines on a good hanging day. And they were happy. They were all special people. They sat on the beach and looked at the sky. A good hanging day, she told them. Nice blue lake, she said.

Rinso white. Rinso blue.

They could hear her now. Every Tuesday after school.

Happy little wash day song.

And they smiled. It was what she wanted. The mint-pink towels, her new yellow stove, her duntes' vases crackled with age and vague with painted flowers swimming over the watery blue surface, slid into view. Pastels (she had conjured them) swam through air to the hazel, blue, green of their eyes. And they smiled; they meant it.

The sunlight shifted to the water's edge. She sat on the beach and smiled, promising herself just one thing. She would sweep them off their feet and carry them, all three, her bundle, her bunch, her sweet potatoes she said, from one spot to another, right there by the water's edge, into the sunlight. She would follow through with it. From sugar to sunlight, from blue vase to the lake (although it wasn't blue, they knew it wasn't), from linen to moonlight. She would see to it, she would get them there, and they would be happy.

She was off somewhere again. They could feel her leaving, with that tilt of her head, with that smile on her face. But the stacked linens, the eye of round, the frosted cake, the lessons in stirring, the kissing of salty skin: this was solid evidence. She had been there once and they sat among the evidence of her days.

Let's go, she said, and they were stepping through sand. She was walking with them to the water's edge. They were here and they were there at home, stepping among her things, hushing through the kingdom of her house. They were in a place of beauty. They had followed her there, their hands groping along some invisible thread she had spun. They were studious, careful, groping along behind her, among the vases, linens, the cakes. They were sifting through sand at the water's edge.

They knew enough. They were cautious. It was many colored. It was hot and cold through their fingers. They were working on it. They were sifting through. She was sad again. She looked at the sky. I take an immense amount of pleasure in my three kids, she said (she almost whispered it, to the wind as much as to them) and hugged her knees. They were sifting through sand, the bright and dark specks. They were digging now, and the bones of their fingers were chilled, digging the warm speckled things.

They would keep it in their minds, the vast stretch of brown sand, the day threatening light then dark. They would keep it for another time, for another place past childhood. Someday they would look back and find themselves ready in buckled shoes, ankle-deep in the shadows of front yard bushes, afraid at the thought of buses, of full sunlight where they didn't want to go, but eager for it too, for the roar of buses over new highways, to be herded in, stepping high, settling in with the smell of baloney sandwiches; and they would find themselves in sunlight, cross-legged on the beach, with the bones of their ankles chilled, burrowed down into wet sand, with a man's black radio burning Buddy Holly into their ears (they laughed, they did); and they would know what they sprang from, where their roots were, spread wide and vast and unresolved, there in the quiet, swirled round with rock 'n' roll, there in the cold, in the hot speckled things.

She sat with them in the sand by the in-and-out water, in the here-and-gone sunlight. Her skin was white and trailed with a delicate leafwork of blue. They worried over her skin. She worried over theirs. She buttoned their shirts. They went to fetch her sweater from the bag and passed the man with the black radio. He was wearing his socks, singing into the air, and they laughed, they jiggled, they danced. They looked to find her again.

She was sitting there alone at the water's edge. They were walking toward her, dragging their feet, trailing her sweater through the wet sand, and the white sleeve dampened and smudged. They hesitated, they ran, they stopped to watch. They let her appear, come into being as they watched. She sat on her ankles. She breathed and rose higher. She was forming herself slowly, bone upon bone, by the water with her too-white skin. With one good breath, then another, she was growing larger and they watched. And someday, they thought, because of water, because of Buddy Holly and Dorothy Avenue, because of miracles and good intentions, because they understood change, because she breathed, she would be lifted, cured, and diving upward, she would laugh, recovered at the sight of something they could not yet see but knew in their own bones as a moment, a flourish in air.

They sat down next to her. And Helen, Eddy, and Lulie Hallissey's definition of heaven fixed itself there in their minds. Heaven was little; it was tribal; it was Anna at the center of their circle of three. It was the days and days with her.

How out of place she seemed in sunlight, braving it for their purposes, clutching her purse. (When it came right down to it, they preferred their room. They liked motels. They liked to belly down on floors, whisper nonsense and kisses into the palms of her hands.)

But they patted the earth for her sake into gateways, into towers. And she was half-hearted. She patted the earth into turrets and smoothed the walls. And no matter what was true, they would make castles. She would poke in the windows. They would trail their fingers along the flat for narrow winding paths. Because she knew that's what they wanted. Because they knew that's what she wanted. A Lake Erie castle: by the dark brown water, she said to herself. By a blue water's edge, they thought later, all tucked into one bed. They would be warm as pennies and imagine it there.

Even in their small room, if it came to that, she would amuse them, she would tell them stories. Listen how the children gallop in their shells, in their pudding bowls and from them, into the streets, into their lives, with the lessons of the woman they lived with. She would take the smallest thing and turn it into a kingdom. She would tell the truth, hold the shell, the cup, the furnished soup ladle to their ears. And in the quiet she would tell them, Listen for the wind. Listen how the ocean lives in our belongings. This storm is in our cups.

Listen, she would tell them, and they would learn. Of the days and days, of surprise departures and arrivals long in coming, of speed, the travel in all things, skyward perhaps or downward, something beyond the touch of their own small fingertips.

She would catch their eye, tug at their sleeves, she would pull them out, into herself, where they wanted to go, where she didn't want to take them, into that dimlit place, into the past. But she would, she would let them, if only for a moment, she would let them come to her, she would take them in. Listen, she would tell them and let them go.

Michael Waters

Scotch and Sun

Home from night shift, my father
was too wired from fighting warehouse fires
to sleep—so he'd sip several Dewar's,
then rouse me for a morning at the beach.
There the combination of scotch and sun
would knock him out for a couple hours
while I invented tasks near the breakage—
skimming clam shells, counting one-legged gulls—
till he woke to hoist me onto his shoulders
and march into the sea, deeper with each step.
He'd look down to find a boy propped there,
his blazing, acceptable burden, his crown, almost
an abstraction shimmering from his skull,
some image of himself he once believed he'd been.
Then arch his neck to shut away the glare.
That noon I leaned too far back, back until my head
dipped into the combers, then below . . .
I struggled, thrashing my legs,
but my father clasped them tighter, closer

to his chest, oblivious, and went on
breasting the rollers, teasing the undertow.
Those broad shoulders eclipsed the sun.
Then hands grasped my hair—I was choking—
while my startled father stammered excuses
to the impromptu chorus of staring bathers.
He was more surprised than I, more scared.
He shook when he told my furious mother.
I simply had no idea, he said. Jesus,
that boy almost drowned
though I held him in my arms.

Moray Eels

Dangerous tinsel, satin slash & slit, green
   ampules of dye spilling through sheer waters,
      the eels unsheathe their phallic flesh from coral
   to tear morsels of manta from the fists of divers
who risk danger for the pleasure of intimate encounter.

To coax them from their crannies,
   the dead skate is wing-grasped, then swished
      like a long-awaited letter from a distant lover
   till the eels, weak-willed, sleek forth
to clamp the flapping bait in traps of teeth.

Sometimes an eel makes a mistake, misjudges
   the wavery inches or, mean-streaked, doesn't,
      and bites the fist that feeds it—an old story,
   another painful lesson as the wound
soon festers with a rare, tropical fungus,

so the few tides after the news fans out
   no tourists tease them from their elkhorn chambers.
      Then, glitzy sleeves of habit, they swivel
   watery passages in search of generous strangers
till their splendor offsets their slender threat

and recent arrivals to the reef
　　resume the tenuous tether to touch another
　　　　creature who, beautiful, may turn on you
　　as lovers sometimes do despite your chummy
motives, deep desires, or all-too-human gestures.

Ambergris Caye
Belize

Driftwood

God's castoff sculpture on the lesser scale:
    forget the riven spines of mountain range or
        rubble-strewn calderas thrust above sea level.
    Been there, done that, He might sigh. And Who
would compete with His own stubborn creation
    wasting a century to spire a single cathedral?
        So He works quickly, having read trendy
    texts on the art of *not-thinking,* those Zen
tea salesmen who honor watchful ancestors
    by pouring ceremonial clouds of steeping
        leaves into tiny, ceramic cups, never
    spilling a drop. One tear brims God's wide eye.
(Severe storm warnings flash along the coast.)
    He has no ancestors due homage, none
        to offer Him some thorny branch of wisdom.
    So He allows His hands to begin their work,
oak after long-standing oak pared to a knobby
    stick, teeth-marked pencil, nubbed
        splinter, then begin again, till
    the coaxed wood issues forth its primeval
soul, the cacophonous score of the creation
    captured in grooves and gnarls. This jazzy
        combo of wind and rain—God's callused palm,

His blunt right thumb—conjures now a tulle
fog beachcombers must part in order to touch
    what's been tossed along the littoral:
        these modest abrasions shape-shifting
    with sand fleas, this rank curvature,
the swirling grain's giddy abstractions
    beckoning the sidewise crabs who vex
        from one knotty installation to the next,
    stalk-eyed critics ragging this tidal
gallery of slathered grit, frothing *no Louise*
    Nevelson while God sips one more scotch.
        Philistines, He fumes, *why do I bother?*
    but He won't return to marble, won't ever
go back to clay—why repeat Himself?
    He knows the artist has no choice
        but to bumble forward, abandoning
    each failure as He abandoned the grand
gesture, these crumbling continents, God's juvenilia.

The Turtles of Santa Rosa

haul their leathery, pock-marked backs
across the ribbed, black marl

like locals rocked with bundles
of tourists' bluejeans and socks.

They deposit their spongy eggs
in pockets gouged in sand,

then turn—so slowly!—
like the hands of wound-down clocks

to rest before dragging
their plosive hearts beyond the breakers.

We prowl with flashlights
and kneel near the nests

to observe the annual ritual
of these hundred-year-old reptiles.

And what can these ancient
washerwomen think of us,

strange creatures generating light,
stepping among the carapaces

while murmuring softly
at the green, instinctual mystery?

Some nights we see their children
struggling from the sands.

Half-conscious, they eye us
on miniature, toy-like oars—

could *we* be their earthly mothers?—
before rowing their way unerringly

toward the ceaseless, nurturing
ululations of the waves.

So I dedicate these words
to the turtles of Santa Rosa

who, a century from now,
on the scrawled floor of the sea,

having grown gentle and enormous,
might then remember me.

Costa Rica, 1985

Susan Minot

The Navigator

In the summer they ate early, everyone drifting home like particles in a tide. By evening most of the people had disappeared from the wharf and the North Eden harbor was quiet, the thorofare running by as flat as a slab of granite. Tonight there was a fog coming in. It was the end of August and all seven of the Vincent children were up there in Maine.

Gus came in off the dock. The screen door ticked out its long yawn, and when he reached the kitchen at the end of the short hall it clapped shut.

The girls were making dinner. Delilah shook salt into the pots on the stove; Sophie peeled a cucumber.

Gus propped his foot against the icebox and bumped against the doorframe.

"Work hard?" Sophie asked.

Gus nodded. He had been house painting all summer; his dark skin was specked with white.

Sophie ran a fork down the side of the cucumber while she held it up next to Gus's face. "For your skin," she said. He closed his eyes to feel the spray.

Delilah folded her arms. "It's just us tonight," she said. "Mum and Dad are going to the Irvings'."

"Dad is?" Gus said. "What is it, skit night?"

"Practically," Sophie said. She picked up a cigarette from the ashtray, took a drag, and gave it to Gus. "They're playing find-the-button."

Gus smiled. "Which one's that?"

"You know. They hide the things—a thimble on the lampshade or a golf tee in the peanuts—the button camouflaged in some flowers. When you spot it, you write it down."

"How'd Mum get him to go?" Gus rubbed the ash into his pants. The bottoms were rolled up in doughnuts.

"God knows," said Sophie.

"It was a choice between that and the Kittredges' clambake on Sunday," Delilah said.

They all laughed.

Delilah was crumbling hamburger. "Poor guy," she said to the frying pan.

"He can handle it," Sophie said.

Gus left them and went into the living room. Chicky, the youngest of the boys, was sitting on the creaking wicker sofa. Going by, Gus swatted the back of his head. On the record player, Bob Dylan was singing "Tangled Up in Blue" for the millionth time. Certain records stayed in North Eden all year long—they were the rejects, hopelessly warped. Still, they got put on again and again. Hearing those songs straight through somewhere else was always a surprise.

Gus took his book off the pile of *National Geographic* and *Harvard* magazines. He stretched out on the window seat, opened the book, and set it facedown on his stomach.

"Went to the quarry," Chicky said. He was whittling at a stick with his Swiss Army knife. "The bottomless one."

"Right," Gus said. He smiled out the window at the floats. The Jewel girls were down there climbing out of their stinkpot. A light mist drifted by in thin trails.

"It was," Chicky said. Shavings littered the floor by his bare feet.

"Chicky, it's impossible," his older brother said. "Quarries're man-made."

Chicky worked over a little knot. "You can think what you want," he said.

From the kitchen, Sophie called, "Where's Minna?" The boys didn't answer. The screen door slammed. "I'm right here," came the six-year-old voice from the hall. Sophie and little Miranda came into the living room at the same time from separate doors.

Sophie said, "Will someone go tell Ma?"

"Is it supper?" Gus asked.

"Five minutes."

"Good," Chicky said.

"Who's going to tell Ma?" Sophie said, holding a stack of napkins at her throat.

Minnie climbed onto Gus's lap and perched on her shins. Gus said, "Minnie will, won't she, Minniana?"

"Do I have to?"

"I would but we're getting supper," Sophie said. She stepped into the dining room but stayed within earshot.

"I always do," said Minnie, collapsing on her brother.

Caitlin walked in. "You always do what?" she asked. Her hair was wet and she hit at it from underneath to dry.

"Well, somebody better go," Sophie said from the dining room. Her head appeared. "Gus, will you?"

Gus winced.

"What?" Caitlin said.

"Why don't you ask Sherman?" Chicky said. He pointed out the window. "He never goes."

Sherman, the middle brother, was standing outside at the dock railing. He was spitting over the edge and watching it land in the water. Someone must have tapped on the window above him—Mum and Dad were upstairs getting dressed—because Sherman turned and looked up. His eyes revealed nothing, like Indian eyes.

"Sure," Sophie said. "Good luck."

Minnie kept her head against Gus's chest. "*He's* not about to get Ma," she said.

"Why not?" Caitlin said. She huffed over to the window and lifted it. A damp mist came rolling over the sill. "Sherman," she said, her voice sounding cottony outside. "Go tell Ma it's supper."

Sherman turned his head. "Why don't you?" he said.

"Because I'm asking you to."

Sherman glanced past her. "Why doesn't Chicky go?" he said.

"I don't believe this," Sophie said.

Chicky's knife peeled a long curl. "She'll come over anyway," he said.

Caitlin turned around to him with her mouth set.

Delilah stood in the doorway with a potholder mitten on. "Has someone gone to get Ma?"

"Gee, Delilah," Gus said. "We thought you'd gone."

"This is ridiculous," Caitlin said. "Come on, Minnie. Go."

Minnie's little back went stiff. "I always do." She shifted off Gus.

"It's not going to kill you," Caitlin said.

Minnie trudged out of the room. They heard the screen door swing, then slam. From where he sat, Gus could see her padding over on the dock to Ma's house. He made a moping face and rocked from side to side, imitating her.

The girls laughed.

THE DINING ROOM had cream-colored walls and two windows that faced the harbor. At high tide, the water rose right up to the shingles and the light made crisscrossing patterns on the low ceiling. It was a small room, just fitting the long table.

Ma, Dad's mother, lived by herself in the far house. Her cook, Livia, had gone back to Ireland, so the kitchen was no longer used. Before supper, Ma read in her living room and had glasses of sherry. By the time she got to the other house for dinner with her grandchildren, her face was flushed.

She sat down, wobbling, at her usual place.

Delilah had a plate at the side table. "Sherman, can you wait? I'm getting this for Ma."

Ma had on a smile. She smiled at the children, smiled at the candle flame, smiled at the blue bowl of grated cheese. "Isn't this nice," she said, smiling. Four small vases of nasturtiums from the garden were on the table.

Gus stood at the window, holding his plate over his chest. "Foggy," he said.

"Is it?" Sophie said. She was busy with wooden spoons in the salad. Everyone bustled around. Caitlin poured milk for Minnie.

Gus nodded and touched his forehead to the pane. "Everything's disappearing," he said.

They'd been eating for a while when Dad came in. He rubbed his hands together. "Evening, evening," he said, shifting from one foot to the other.

"You look pretty snappy," Sophie said. He was wearing a yellow blazer and a tie with green anchors on it. His face looked freshly slapped.

"Mum assures me I won't be allowed in Lally Irving's house without the proper attire," he said, bent slightly at the waist.

"You look great," Caitlin said.

Dad smiled dismissively.

Mum came in smelling of perfume, wearing a long skirt. "See you later, monkeys," she said. She plucked a carrot stick from the salad.

Ma beamed at Mum. "Rosie," she said.

Mum's real name was Rose Marie—it was Irish—but she'd changed it, thanks to Dad. He called her Rosie after the schoolteacher in *The African Queen* who dumps out all of Humphrey Bogart's gin in order to get them down the river. Mum never drank at all.

She looked at her family in the candlelight. "Okey-dokey," she said.

"Good luck finding the button," Gus said.

"Who needs luck?" Mum said, kicking out her foot. "You're looking at last year's champ. Come on, Uncs, off we go."

Dad bowed, putting his palms together, and followed after her. Everyone at the table chuckled. Ma was smiling. She held her fork over her plate but still had not touched her food.

EARLY THE NEXT MORNING Gus woke up the boys to explain what had happened.

"They got home from the Irvings'," Gus said, "and Mum couldn't get him down the steps."

There were five flights of granite that led down from the street. Gus and the girls had heard Mum call "Yoo hoo." Gus went up the steps to help Dad down. The girls stood in the floodlight of the underpass, watching in the fog. Gus and Mum brought him into the light. Collapsed between them, Dad had been smiling grandly. He caught sight of his daughters in a semicircle and beamed toward them. Receiving no response, he had made a *whoops* expression and covered his mouth, giggling.

Gus sat on Sherman's bed but faced Chicky. "We're going to talk to him this morning," he said.

"What for?" Sherman said. "Let the guy do what he wants."

The girls were downstairs with Mum, except for Minnie, who was at sailing class.

"He didn't want to go in the first place," Mum said, washing dishes at the sink. "I shouldn't have made him."

Caitlin waited by the toaster. "What happened?" she asked.

"He was okay till dinner," Mum said. She gazed through the window in front of her; the shingles of the house next door were a foot away. "Then halfway through the roast beef he decided he was finished and plopped his plate down on top of Mrs. Aberdeen's."

They all smiled in spite of themselves.

"What did Mrs. Aberdeen do?" Delilah said.

Mum shook her head.

Caitlin was serious. "Then what?"

"He collapsed on his place mat with his hands over his head." Mum turned to her daughters. "He said, 'This is so *boring.*'"

Caitlin was still. "You're kidding."

"Then—" Mum took a breath. "Everyone pretended it was time to go and they put their jackets back on and we all said good-bye and they helped Dad find his way to the car. After we drove off, I imagine they went back in and finished dinner."

Sophie said, "You mean they faked going home?"

Mum shrugged: that was nothing.

The boys were shuffling in. Mum said, "He won't listen to me. I'm like a buzz in his ear."

They waited at the table, the girls at the near end, the boys next to the windows.

Sophie heard Dad and set down her knife. Delilah straightened her spine. Dad came in with his plate and put it down. Caitlin bit delicately into her muffin, stealing glances in Dad's direction. Dad went back into the kitchen and returned with a carton of orange juice. He poured a glass and drank it standing up.

Mum was beside him, holding the back of her chair. Her scarf was rolled into a hair band above her wide forehead. She had on a lavender turtleneck.

"The kids want to talk to you, Uncs," she said and slipped into her seat.

Dad pulled out his chair noisily. He buttered his toast, not waiting for the butter to melt. "You ready for a little golf today, Sherman?" he said, not looking up.

Gus looked at Sherman, then at his father, then at Mum. Mum was pressing crumbs with her fingers and brushing them off, making a little pile. Chicky was interested in something under the table. He made a noise to call the cat. Sherman sat heavily, no breakfast plate in front of him, his hands in his lap.

Caitlin spoke first. "Do you remember last night?"

Dad's chin traced out a long nod.

"How's your arm?" Delilah asked.

"My hand," he said and held it up. "Stiff." He put it back down and with his good hand folded some toast around his bacon and took a bite.

Halfway down the steps, he had broken free of Gus and Mum and keeled over into the unguarded rubble. There had been a trickling of small stones after him. The girls watched helplessly as he got onto his hands and knees. His head had wobbled like one of those toy dogs people have on their dashboards. The girls looked away.

"Dad, do you remember talking to me?" Gus said.

"Yes," said his father, addressing the jar of beach-plum jelly before him.

"What?" Delilah said.

Dad's frown was like a twitch. "Yes," he repeated.

"Do you remember what you said you'd do?" Gus asked.

Dad dipped his rolled-up toast into his mug of coffee. He nodded.

"Well?" Caitlin said. "What about it?"

Dad chewed, keeping his mouth closed. He looked around the table with an innocent expression.

Sophie said, "We have to talk about it."

"Fine," he said.

While Gus was bringing him upstairs, the girls had lingered in the hall with Mum. Above them, they heard Gus's urgent voice. They sat on the bottom step, transfixed. His voice was pleading, "We all do . . . because whenever we try . . . can't stand it when you . . ."

Outside some footsteps had banged by—two figures in yellow slickers passed the doorway—their steps ringing woodenly on the dock. But the girls hardly noticed, glancing over like sleepwalkers. The fog blew by through the underpass.

Above them they had heard Dad say, "Imagine that."

Caitlin covered her knuckles and slouched forward on the table. "So will you stop?" She looked at Mum. Mum was gazing out the window.

Dad looked at Caitlin as if she were speaking another language.

Sophie said, "You have to, Dad," and her voice wavered. Dad turned to her with the same face, blank but suspecting insult.

"Well?" Caitlin said.

Chicky pointed toward the water. "Look," he said.

Everyone turned. A huge green cattle boat had entered the window frame, undulating behind the tiny streaks in the glass. The white sails were as flat as building sides. It changed the light in the dining room.

"Looks like the *Horn of Plenty*," Mum said brightly.

Everyone watched it glide into the second window.

"No," Sherman said. It was a mystery how he knew these things. "That's *Captain's Folly*."

When Dad was young he had worked summers on a cattle boat that cruised through the islands. He'd been the navigator. He still had an astronomy book on the bottom shelf of his bedside table.

"Is it anchoring?" Sophie asked.

Delilah shook her head. "It's just passing through."

The sailboat slipped out of the window frame. Gus tipped back his chair to keep it in sight. It continued through the thorofare. At the outer cove, its sails buckled and a tiny figure at the bow lowered a huge anchor into the water. Gus set his chair down and faced back in.

Dad hit the table with his hand like a gavel and started to get up.

"Wait," Caitlin said. "Dad." His frown was attentive. She ducked and went on, "We think you need help."

Dad glanced at Mum. She was fiddling with her pearl earring. Her other hand came up for an adjustment.

"You do, Dad," Sophie said.

Dad's gaze went over the table—the green vases of red nasturtiums, some Sugar Pops casting pebble shadows.... He reached into his pocket, hitching up his whole side as if mounting a horse. "Okay," he said uncertainly. He brought out a pack of cigarettes and stirred his finger in the opening. When he lit one, it burned halfway down in the first drag.

Sophie covered her forehead. "Okay what?" she said.

Dad looked at her with a cold eye. Delilah nudged her; she kept facing Dad. His posture was stiff and erect and his lips were pressed smartly together.

Caitlin lifted her chin toward him. "Okay what?" she said.

His eyes glared. She shrank back. As he put out his cigarette, his throat seemed to swell, as if his Adam's apple were expanding and the whole of his uncomfortable being were struggling there in his throat. He coughed. "I won't drink," he said.

Was that it? Caitlin began to smile. Sophie picked up a muffin crust and tapped it on her plate.

Gus said, "But, Dad, do you think—?"

"I said, 'I won't drink.'"

"I know, but..." Gus inspected his hands lying flat in front of him. Delilah said, "That's great, Dad."

Dad's chair scraped the floor and he stood up. Mum had a satisfied face. "Okay, monkeys," she said, "where shall we take the picnic?"

THE SKY WAS SMOOTH, blue and clear. Ma watched from her balcony while they streamed out to the boat. A book lay in her lap. She had stopped going on picnics. Each one said good-bye to her, passing beneath her with their towels and books and baskets. Ma held a cigarette pinched elegantly between thumb and finger. The skirt of her print dress stirred against the chair.

Random River was at the end of one of the coves that scalloped off the thorofare. A tidal river, it was a muddy bed dotted with boulders at low tide. When the tide was high, a boat could motor up there. Even then, rocks appeared, just breaking the surface.

Dad stood at the wheel of the fiber-glass motorboat. His seven children were arranged in various perches; the motor gurgled at a slow speed. Mum sat beside him behind the windshield with her round sunglasses on. Usually there was much advice about the rocks, or Dad would appoint a lookout. "You're heading right for one!" "No no! To the left!" Today, there wasn't a peep. Dad navigated his way down the swirling turns, over the dimpled water.

It was glassy along the shore, the water dark green and shaded, bugs leaving pinpricks here and there. Bristling out of the rocks was the stiff grass—a porous leaf that slashed your calves when you were wading. There were tiny slugs clinging to the blades.

The Vincents glided toward their rock. They always went to the same rock. It had a plateau where the picnic basket got put and a scooped-out place where you could lie in the sun. In the photo albums there were lots of pictures taken here.

Gus stepped over the bow railing and crouched at the front.

"Careful," Mum said.

He leapt onto the rock and turned to fend off the bow.

"Eggshell landing," Caitlin said.

They all felt the crunch. "Whoops," Sophie said. But nothing was going to disturb the dreamy contentment that had taken over.

They unloaded, balancing cushions and coolers, lowering Minnie by her armpits. Delilah gripped Mum's arm while she stepped down.

At the stern, Dad flung the anchor into the water. Gus led the painter into a jumble of rocks.

The sun streaked across the long ripples of the lagoon. Had Ma been there, she'd have already been in. Sophie tested the water. Everyone moved about politely. Caitlin squinted into the sun, then laid out her towel. She tugged the towel over to make room for Sophie. Mum pulled Minnie's sweatshirt over her head and her pigtails popped out.

"Listen to this," Delilah said. She had a magazine across her thighs. "'The two hundred couples exchanged vows beneath a grape bower on the Reverend's California estate.'"

"Sick," Mum said. She settled her head back on Minnie's life jacket.

"'Afterwards, the wedded devotees reaffirmed their faith in a baptismal ceremony in the garden fountains.'"

"Unbelievable," Caitlin said.

Sherman was rummaging around in the picnic basket. He stood up with a handful of Fritos and crunched them one at a time. Dad carried the cooler up higher into the shade. There was a toppled tree up there, with roots that spread in a fan. When they were younger, the kids used to stand in front of it and hoot and listen for the echo. It was like a half-shell, the way the sounds reverberated. Up close, the roots and moss made intricate designs, like an ancient chart. Chicky was digging at a groove in the rock with a stick, idly but persistently. Gus and Minnie squatted over some curly black lichen. "Indian cornflakes," Gus said. Minnie laughed. It was quiet and pleasant and there was no noise except the drone of a motorboat somewhere out on the water.

Then they all heard the sound.

They sometimes heard noises far off—a *crack* like that—someone with a shotgun who knew what he was doing, or a pickup backfiring on the South Eden bridge farther down the river. But none of the picnickers mistook this sound.

Some heads jerked toward Dad; some looked down. Above them, Dad was facing the root screen, his back to the family. Mum didn't move, lying on the life jacket, eyes hidden behind her sunglasses. Sophie hugged her shins and bit her knee. Gus's neck was twisted into a tortured position; he glared at Dad's back.

Dad turned around. He gazed with an innocent expression out over the snaking water. If aware of the eyes upon him, Dad did not betray it, observing the scenery with contentment; nothing more normal than for him to be standing in the shade at a family picnic holding a can of beer. He twisted the ring from its opening and, squinting at a far-off view, stooped to lap up the nipple of foam at the top of the can.

The silence was no longer tranquil.

Sometimes on still, black nights they had had throwing contests off the dock. They threw stones into the thorofare and listened to hear them land. Sometimes the darkness would swallow up a stone and they'd wait, but no sound would come. It seemed then as if the stone had gone into some further darkness, entered some other dimension where things went on falling and falling.

Shara McCallum

The Fisherman's Wife

Each day I will make you
a meal of fish heads soaked
in scallions, scotch bonnets, vinegar
and wine; cassava pounded flat
beneath my fists, then fried crisp;
roasted plantains; soursop juice
teased with lime. At dusk
before your return, I will
bathe in rosewater, oil my scalp,
polish my skin till it glistens
in the coming moonlight
like mother-of-pearl washed ashore.

In time, you will forget
the painted dusk calling you back;
the surf rupturing herself again and again
for the sand's fleeting touch;
the flamboyant sun rising
from beneath the ocean's shell:

her heat swirling across your face
like Salome's last veil come undone.

What the stories teach:

The man playing the flute
always gets what he wants:
unsuspecting babes
forsake trikes, toss dolls
face down in the dirt, leave
mommy and daddy's good night
kiss and tuck to dust.
Skipping and singing into the silent sea,
the last head descends into the water
the way an apple vanishes
beneath the caramel glaze.

Debora Greger

Sea Change

Minus tide. In an old coat but barefoot,
I trailed across sand flats
into a luminous fog. What wet light—
a thick glow that failed to illuminate,

a clarity so circumscribed I thought
of old theories: the earth a dish
balanced on a dozen columns
or the back of a turtle. What use

were such notions? Held in the right light,
they could have reflected the holder,
like the dream you had after your wife's
sudden death—that she had instead

taken a lover. You seemed to take
some comfort in this change of pains,
said you preferred it to the dream
of walking this stretch, feet stung with cold,

lungs damp, and following in mind's eye
someone whose familiar gait swiftly
outdistanced your memory.
The world does have edges beyond which

the dead lie, in another element,
like the deep fish that, dragged to the surface,
explode. Even sea salt, its sweaty,
womanly pungency could conjure

nothing sympathetic. *Memento mori,*
that's what it becomes, rime of decay
on the water's detritus. Shallow bowls
of sand have caught the offerings:

little crab under a chipped whelk, half
a ragged scallop shell, bottleneck crusted
with limpets, shard of a bisque doll's face
abraded until featureless.

The Shallows

Rolling pants' legs, bundling skirts,
they have come down the shore with gunny sacks,

bird cages, dresses knotted together—
tonight not the moon but a run of smelt

silvers the shallows, night water's deep opacity.
Gray gone black, the wet sand chills, floor-hard

as long as, like those boys, I don't stand still.
Coaching and taunting, a chorus of spring frogs,

they leap the fish. Even the woman I've seen
walking daily in the village is here, the one

with her arm in a sling and a three-legged dog.
Her slowed passage rippling the crowd,

she's the domestic tamely obscured
by the raucous dark. Down from this inlet,

a basket of lights lists where the family living
on the grounded freighter finishes another

tilted day. Finally, I think, that canted home
would seem no longer maddening or novel

but cramped like any other. Out in its vast
and watery front yard, below the level of all this,

a cold current tunnels unremittingly north.

Tom Horton

The Greatest Poets

The dawn comes up windy, shuddering the bedroom window. Senses kick in behind shut eyelids, divining the day's priorities from a puff of air. How hard is it blowing? From what direction? If it's southeast, better get out to the dock and drop the stern line on the skiff and let it swing, or it could swamp; and all my neighbors will likely be home early from work—easterlies make the crabs they seek bury out of reach in the bottom. Northwest? If it maintains from that direction, the tides won't make up high at all; forget any thoughts of taking the big workboat in shoal water tomorrow. Northeast? Sleep in. Cancel the pediatrician. The ten-mile run to Crisfield on the mainland would be just too rough and wet for a sick kid.

When you live and work on an island, you play these little chess games with Nature continuously. You become attuned, almost subliminally, to the winds and moon phases, to the ebb and flood of water and the lengthening and shortening of the days. And then you leave, one late-summer day, for the mainland, for the dream home you have bought, spacious and modern in a quiet, leafy suburb—good schools, neat playgrounds, near to major malls. Life there is so very much more convenient and predictable and controllable. Soon, you don't even notice the wind outside your bedroom window.

IN 1987 MY WIFE, Cheri, and I decided to move to Smith Island, a fishing community of about five hundred souls in the middle of Chesapeake Bay. We rented our Baltimore row house for enough to cover the mortgage and took the two kids out of private schools. I would run environmental education trips for the Chesapeake Bay Foundation, which owned an old island house with twenty bunk beds. It meant a pay cut of about $35,000 a year from our mainland jobs (I a reporter, Cheri a social worker). Perhaps it seemed strange in Ronald Reagan's America of the eighties, with its emphasis on upward mobility of the most materialistic stripe; but in the midst of a prospering journalism career, I felt a need to shrink my prospects, narrow my horizons, and move on to smaller endeavors. As an environmental reporter I trekked through Amazonian rainforests, followed famine across Africa, and researched ozone destruction above Antarctica; but my roots were deep in less fabulous places.

A long time before I came to write about the overarching environmental issues of our day; well before I discovered Thoreau, John Muir, Aldo Leopold, and the other great naturalist-philosophers—before all that I just liked to muck around in the marshes of my native Chesapeake. I fished those soggy edges for striped bass, hunted the potholes for black duck, slogged through the clingiest black ooze this side of quicksand, and combed the wracklines for driftwood. I loved to hear the pock and slurp of waves in the marsh's honeycombed banks, to whiff the robust flatulence of its decaying organic matter, and watch sun and moon work filigrees of gold and silver on intricate braids of water and grass. To anyone who wondered how I trained as an environmental writer, the most meaningful answer was that I grew up liking to muck in the marsh.

John Steinbeck, in *The Log from the Sea of Cortez*,* wrote of his expedition collecting marine life along the shores of the Gulf of California: *"It is advisable to look from the tide pool to the stars and then back to the tide pool again."* What he meant was that we can spend the next ten thousand years identifying individual creatures and dissecting them down to the level of the gene and the atom, and we may similarly roll back the curtains of heaven itself with our telescopes and spaceships; but the fullest wonder lies in comprehending nature's patterns, the wondrous webs of interdependence that entangle humankind in all creation, above and below. Smith Island, whose marshbound residents for about three centuries have paid serious attention to both God and crabs, and where the little white villages on clear, calm days float magically between sea and sky, seemed well stationed to observe tidepool and stars alike; and my kids were reaching marsh-mucking age.

SO IT WAS THAT IN THE SPRING of '87 we moved to the town of Tylerton, last stop on the ferry, unfrequented even by the tour boats to the island's other two communities. The population of 124 was mostly descended from English and Welsh colonists who came here beginning in the late 1600s. Half the town was named either Marshall or Bradshaw; also fourteen Tylers, thirteen Corbins; smatterings of Smiths, Marshes, Tulls, Evanses, and Lairds—and now, for the first time in history, four Hortons.

I took a house that had stood for 170 years, said to be the oldest on the island. It occupied a little peninsula of lawn—rare as emerald

---

* New York, Viking Press, 1969.

in those low-lying and salty environs. Huge old hackberry trees that shaded it bore every spring and fall a bonus crop of migrant warblers, orioles, tanagers, and vireos, glad for a rest on their way to and from the tropics. Every window and door had a view you would pay serious money for on the mainland, and there were thirty-six of them. That nearly half of these faced broadside to the North Pole would not strike us until our first winter.

My street, really just a path, had no name. With only sixty-seven houses and centuries of close acquaintance, islanders had never thought addresses too important. This gave United Parcel Service fits, and Federal Express and the *Baltimore Sun* circulation departments refused to deal with it at all. If you are not at a certifiable point on somebody's grid, in modern America you scarcely exist; so we made up our own addresses. As the mood struck, we resided on Water Street and Waterview Boulevard, Harbourview and Horton Pike. A friend once addressed me thus: "Tom Horton, His Own Way." Connie, our postmistress, took it all in stride. She knew where we all were.

We also resided "Up Above," as opposed to those Tylertonians who lived "Down Below," and this distinction was important. Assignments at PTA, Ladies Aid, and such were made on this basis, as in: "Up Above brings the meat dishes this time, and Down Below makes the desserts; all pitch in on the salads." Another island village was grouped into "Down the Field" and "Over the Hill." The whole island is nearly flat as a billiard table, and I once asked to be shown the "hill." Well, everyone knows sort of where it runs . . . maybe it has gotten wore down over all this time, people said.

Half a minute's walk either way along my street, or most any other in Tylerton, would land you in the water. It was a great part of what so charmed visitors when they first saw the island towns as the boat from the mainland neared the island—that they just ended, rather than bleeding off in the scattered jumble of strip development and suburbia that so uglifies much of the mainland. This abrupt edge between civilization and nature seemed less confining than you might think. The sun and moon rose at one end of my humble street and set at the other; and from where the pavement stopped the view stretched unimpeded, westward toward the mouth of the Potomac River; eastward across Tangier Sound and the vast prairies of salt marsh along Maryland's Eastern Shore. From my front door I could skip an oyster shell into the true Main Street of Tylerton, the channel of Tyler's Creek.

Everything entered and departed town this way: the ferry, the preacher making his Sunday rounds; crabs migrating, stingrays spawning; also sea ducks, black skimmers, diamondback terrapins, and the occasional shark. Between the channel edge and my front yard, egrets, herons, and gulls progged the shallow, submerged grass beds for soft crabs and minnows and grass shrimp. Here, the ancient territories of animals still overlapped, maintained some semblance of balance with the territory of humankind. One morning I watched a great blue heron battle a great black-backed gull two hours for a huge eel speared on the former's marlinspike bill. The eel proved the toughest customer, finally eluding both birds. Once an otter, the most secretive of marsh dwellers, loped onto my lawn and watched as I mowed grass.

One image is especially savory: Hand in hand, I walked Abby, six, down the lane back to the one-room school that served pre-K through sixth grade. Hot, early-autumn sunshine simmered down through the hackberries that had arched this path for centuries. Odors of steaming crab mingled with mown grass and the faint perfumes of salt and creosote that cling to older waterfronts. Overhead, Canada geese called, and in the shallows snowy egrets sipped minnows delicately. A lone crab, an escapee from the steaming pot, scuttled from under a building and preceded us down the path, dancing sidewise, seeking saltwater. It recalled Thomas Hardy's description of an English village so rural that "a butterfly might have wandered down the main street without interruption." Abby skipped along. So did I.

Tourists who take the half-day boat ride and seafood lunch special to Smith Island generally think the place unique, but ultimately dull and monotonous overall. There is in fact little variety in the vegetation of the tidal marsh that covers all but a few of the 8,000 acres here. Few plants on earth have evolved to tolerate salt, and the Chesapeake here—about halfway in miles and in salt content between the ocean at its mouth and its river-dominated headwaters—permits fewer species than flourish in even the meanest woodlot on the mainland. The marsh is amply compensated, however, because those few plants that can pass salt's stern muster grow like gangbusters in the nutrient-rich broth swishing hourly through their roots on the ebb and flood of the tides. The marsh may never draw aesthetic favor away from New England hillsides in autumn, but it is among the most productive of earth's natural systems, guilelessly surpassing all but the most energy- and labor-intensive applications of human agriculture. This is all well documented in the literature of ecology, and doctrine by now to generations of environmentalists. But there is more to marshiness than science—or even art and literature—has documented. Like so much about Smith Island, it does not shout its virtues, but yields them only to probing and observation.

A marsh-clad island is a place alive. It ripples sleekly beneath the wind's stroking, altering mood and texture with every caress and pummel. Its salty sameness stretches a perfect artist's linen beneath the sky, a playground for the romp of light, and exquisitely responsive to every shift of sun and season and weather. A thousand channels and cricks and guts rive the marsh, and through them the bay perfuses Smith Island like some great, amorphous jellyfish. And these watery thoroughfares, the main means of travel within the island, do something quite profound. They seldom run straight for long. They curve. I doubt George Santayana, the philosopher, ever went "gut running," an island sport that consists of racing one's skiff through the fantastic maze of loops and whorls and meanders the marshways make. But he would have understood the thrill. In his classic treatise on form in *The Sense of Beauty* (1896), Santayana wrote of the pleasure we take from the curved line: "*at every turn reawakening, with a variation, the sense of the previous position . . . such rhythms and harmonies are delightful.*"

For one accustomed to the straight and the angle of mainland road travel, moving through the island's arteries is at first disorienting. Landmarks are sparse—three villages and half a dozen hammocks of trees spread across twenty square miles of low marsh and interior waters. Your angle of orientation changes continuously. Leaving Tylerton, one moment the town is holding reassuringly off one shoulder; the next it has hunkered down out of sight behind a hammock; then it reappears, broadside, all its homes in view and looking larger than life, only to begin contracting. The landforms seem conspiring to trick you—merging, hiding, elongating; from unexpected directions, *pouncing.*

Ultimately this physical and psychological to-and-fro becomes deeply stimulating, even sensuous. One contemplates the island's shape-shifting as you might slowly rotate a crystal, regarding familiar objects embedded within from an infinity of perspectives. Straight lines may never be proven inherently inferior, but from galaxies to the shells of whelks, it does seem the bent of the universe to orbit, oscillate, cycle and spiral, to meander and to turn.

Whorled and whirled may be the way of the world, and of Smith Island; but "flat" would be your first impression of the place. We had been there for months when I mentioned on an evening walk to Cheri how remarkably the lights of Tangier, half a dozen miles across the water, were twinkling in the clear air. What lights? she said. She had never seen them. It struck me then that she is five feet nine and I am six feet six. The additional elevation lent a whole different view. This flatness extended far beyond and below the visible island, radiating for miles in every direction along the most gentle of underwater slopes. What looked to be a limitless quantity of water surrounding us was in fact extraordinarily *thin*, ranging in depth from inches to a few feet. This shallowness fundamentally shaped islands and islanders. Sunlight easily penetrates to the bottom in these skinny waters, growing lush meadows of aquatic vegetation that attract nearly every type of fish and fowl associated with the Chesapeake Bay.

Prominent among these is the savory blue crab, of which the bay yields more than 100 million pounds annually. Crabs must periodically shed their hard, spiny shells to grow; also, in the females' case, in order to mate. When soft, they are a delicacy and quite valuable. This molting and mating occurs each summer throughout the blue crab's range, from Texas to Long Island; but it is more concentrated and accessible than perhaps anywhere on earth in the grass beds within a twenty-mile radius of Smith Island. Islanders, who depend absolutely for their being on harvesting the soft crab, are connected to the grasses and the bay's essential shallowness as intimately as stalking herons or speckled trout cruising the submerged jungles for prey.

Here, within a day's drive of some 50 million moderns, exists a culture exquisitely attuned to its natural surroundings as only predators can be. "Left or right?" I asked an old neighbor lady one day as I fumbled to turn the burner on her gas stove to light it. "Turn it east, honey," she replied. I got similar instructions on a construction project. "Drive that nail more to nor'west." Even the phone exchange here, HA5, came from Hazel, the big hurricane that devastated the place back in the 1950s.

You could track the progress of crabbing just as accurately through the collections at the Methodist church as through any landing statistics kept by the state. In May, when the first big crab run hit Tyler's Creek, money put in the offering plate might go in a week from $200 to more than $2,000, on attendance of about forty persons.

Just as the elemental, chameleon marsh seemed at first glance monotonous, the fishing life of the islanders also struck outsiders as dreary and repetitious. In fact, every day demanded a complex assessment of tide and temperature, wind and changing season, and a dozen other considerations—many more felt than articulated—that would influence where to work, for how long, in what manner, and how much income there would be. It was physically hard, often uncertain to the point of overstress; but seldom uninteresting. Life on the mainland came to seem predictable by contrast. A shift in the breeze scarcely ever affects where one will sell insurance, or dictates how much paper can be shuffled by day's end.

STRICTLY SPEAKING, you do not actually move to Smith Island. No post office by that name exists or ever has. One moves to Ewell, the "capital city" of about 250, or to Rhodes Point, at the end of the island's only true road, extending two miles across the marsh from Ewell; or one goes to Tylerton, the smallest and most isolated community, reachable from the other towns only by water.

Rhodes Point, they will tell you in Ewell, was called *Rogues* Point until a century or so ago for good reason, the implication being that some of the roguishness lingers yet. Ewell, say the Tylertonians, is noisier (with maybe forty cars to Tylerton's couple), and is just a tad full of itself. As for Tylerton, well that is where the "holy rollers" still hold sway, where the Methodist religion, which is taken right seriously in all three towns, predominates most. Life there, feel people in Ewell and Rhodes Point, must be unbearably small town and dull. Over the centuries, things have gotten pretty well sorted out. I doubt you could muster a skiffload of islanders who have the slightest desire to move from the town where they live into one of the others.

Moving to Smith Island was not such a dislocation for me. I grew up on Maryland's Eastern Shore, close to the Chesapeake and its marsh islands. But Cheri was from Salt Lake City, and had never lived outside cities. As for Abigail, six, and Tyler, nine, they had grown up playing in Baltimore alleyways. The closest they usually got to water was the storm drain. How would they fit with the kids of crabbers and fishermen?

The enormity of it hit one steamy June day as I prepared for the family's arrival. The house was an oven. The church had asked that even our single downstairs air conditioner be turned off: the pumps the crabbers used to keep water flowing over their catch needed all the available electricity. Clouds of biting insects swarmed outside. From under the kitchen, a rat, perhaps the only thing my wife hated more than bugs, was gnawing away. What had I done, committing my family to some personal dream of living on an island in the bay?

We were liberal, big-city Democrats. Tylerton was red-white-and-blue conservative. Cheri and the kids are Catholics, and Smith Island uniformly practiced a staunch and fundamentalist brand of Methodism. If you want to talk evolution, make sure you smile when you say it. The island has never opted for local government in its centuries of settlement. There are no jails, no police, no mayor, no town council. The church, to a greater extent than anywhere else in America, fills the role of government. If we didn't fit in, little Tylerton could become confining indeed.

The day before Cheri and the kids were to join me, a woman from down the street stopped by to chat. She came bearing the traditional Smith Island welcoming gift, an eight-layer cake. She said how glad everyone was to see our family moving in. Then she said something that I thought at the time was quaint—perhaps an island way of speaking. "It's so good to see your lights at night." It would be months later before I understood fully—and sorrowfully—what she meant.

That first summer on the island was instant paradise for Tyler. He was off fishing in a skiff with a couple islanders before he had unpacked all his bags. He roamed the town and adjoining marshes at will with the island kids. Lest this sound like stepping into a Huck Finn tale, I should add he also spent hours glued to the video games at the Tylerton store, and pestered us endlessly for a Nintendo like one of his compatriots had. Abby, shyer than her big brother, stuck closer to home; but it was not long before she was out on the dock with a buddy, enticing baitfish into a Mason jar filled with bread and dangled by a string into the water. "Minner, minner, come get your dinner," they sang, and fed their catch to the local cats.

Those first weeks were toughest for Cheri. I had my job, taking groups of schoolkids around the bay and marshes. The kids had playmates. "Mom, why can't you pick [crabs] like the other ladies?" Tyler asked. All Mom's skills as a clinical social worker seemed worthless here. She was welcomed, but she had landed on one of earth's greatest seafood plantations at high harvest season. The income crabs provide between May and September is the great bulk of the year's money for most islanders, and both men and women are feverishly devoted to catching and processing the crustaceans, rising early as 2:00 A.M. and going until 9:00 P.M., six days a week. Only their religion stops them every seventh day. The pace was so frantic, it seemed if the church hadn't stopped them, the people would have had to invent another reason to take a break, or risk burning out by the Fourth of July. It wasn't only the islanders who needed the rest, a waterman said. "The crabs need a break, too." And Monday morning was nearly always the best catch of the week.

Summer's bugs were vanishing before the frosts, the frenzy of crabbing season was slacking off, and Cheri's spirits were picking up. She was busy with PTA and helping out the Methodist ladies with church suppers. In a town the size of Tylerton, everyone's help is needed. We felt valued in a way rarely experienced on the mainland. If islands, by definition, isolate, then they also amplify their residents' sense of community. "It ain't much to look at, but we're close," a crabber said to me. Slowly but surely, we were forming bonds with people whose different cultural and educational backgrounds would, on the mainland, have segregated us surely as concrete barriers. Shortly after the *Exxon Valdez* had spewed oil across Alaska's Prince William Sound, I was leaving to cover the disaster for *Rolling Stone* magazine when Tyler came back from evening church. "They prayed for you tonight, Dad, that you come back all right." I had an insane urge to fax *Rolling Stone*: "Trust the staff there is praying for my success in this difficult endeavor."

With the Halloween Social approaching, Cheri was asked to bake a cake for the traditional cakewalk. This is played something like musical chairs. You plunk down a quarter and walk to music around a circle of numbered sections chalked on the wooden floor of the community hall. If the music stops and leaves you on the number that is drawn, you win the cake. Now cakes are treated on the island only slightly less seriously than crabs. You are offered eight-layer cake in Tylerton routinely as people on the mainland brew visitors a cup of instant coffee. No one expected Cheri to produce one of these masterpieces, but she felt less than three layers would be laughed at. The old kitchen floor tilted south to north, and so did her first efforts at a cake. She went next door to the kitchen where we housed the kids on educational tours; there she produced a cake that slanted east to west. By now there was nothing to do but make the icing as thick as possible, slap the layers together, and try to refrigerate the whole mess to a gluey integrity by showtime.

"You bring the cake, and for God's sake don't let it slide apart," she said as the time for the social arrived. I opened the refrigerator. One layer was in the back corner; another layer was in another corner; the third had begun to slide down the back of the refrigerator between the shelves. As it turned out, it was a blessing in disguise. At the social, we realized that the islanders, who could be incredibly gentle and sensitive, were the severest of cake critics. Each cake was cut in half and displayed before the circle formed for the cakewalk. "Nah, I wouldn't risk a quarter for that one," I heard as a gorgeous specimen was paraded around; and only a few people walked to the music. I kept thinking, what if we had brought a cake to the cakewalk and nobody walked? It would have been the ultimate humiliation—worse than wearing your oilskins tucked so they drain inside your hip boots.

My own work of motivating schoolkids to "Save the Bay" was going well. Few if any islanders thought of their community as an incredible educational tool; but on the final day of a field trip, I would play an ace that seldom failed, relying on the kids' inevitable fascination with Smith Island. On a large map that covered parts of six states, we would travel from the tiny island north to Cooperstown, New York; westward out across the Blue Ridge and Shenandoahs into West Virginia; and south almost into North Carolina. All that immense land, nearly a sixth of the eastern seaboard between Maine and Georgia, lay within the drainage basin, or *watershed*, of the Chesapeake Bay, I would tell them. What that meant was that everything humans in those 64,000 square miles did to pollute, from felling forests and farming destructively to flushing toilets and bombarding their lawns with chemicals—all of that was eventually carried by rainfall and forty-odd rivers downstream to the Chesapeake.

Ultimately, the most important grade for our civilization would be how well we achieved a long-term, stable accommodation between nature and human numbers that grew without limit. The Chesapeake was as good a final exam as anywhere on earth—a world-class resource, polluted big time, and now the object of unprecedented restoration efforts, even as population in its watershed burgeoned from 15 million to 18 million in the next few decades. Literally in the center of this struggle lay little Smith Island, some 500 souls totally dependent on a healthy natural environment, downstream from the other 15–18 million of us. If you go away from here remembering only one lesson, I would tell the kids, make it this: How responsibly you live back home helps determine whether this place survives. There were very few skulls and hearts that pitch did not penetrate.

WINTER HIT HARD and fast that first year on the island. The big nor'westers came screaming down Tangier Sound with nothing to impede them for thirty miles of open water and marsh before they slammed broadside into our uninsulated house, which had no central heat. We used to sit, huddled under blankets in the living room, watching the mainland weather mention "winds 6 to 12 knots, variable," while the house rocked in the grip of 30 knots and gusting. We began keeping items like salad oil in the refrigerator so they wouldn't freeze overnight.

If winters could be harsh, they always started well because of the Christmas holidays. Christmas is a big deal on Smith Island, and Christmas lights are an especially big deal. "You are going to put up lights," a neighbor told us, friendly but firm. It was the only time I can ever recall being *told* to do anything in this place where independence is valued nearly to the point of anarchy. I was never big on Christmas festivities, to Cheri's everlasting despair; but I managed a few cheap strings of lights, tucked into some cedar branches that I and the kids cut from the big heron rookery in a hammock out on the marsh. Everyone's lights looked great. They helped to disguise the fact that the town had been growing darker, and not just from the shortening days.

The "Save the Bay" house had been closed up for the winter. The few summer residents were gone until spring; and some of the older widows had left to live with children in Ewell or on the mainland until the weather warmed again. We went away the week after Christmas, returning in early January. One night, I walked outside. It was drizzly, a fog was rolling up Tangier Sound. Swans bayed like lost souls in the blackness down by Horse Hammock Point. The foghorn moaned out by the jetties above Ewell. All the

Christmas lights were gone now. On my street, only three of seven houses had lights on. The other four were empty, or inhabited only by summer people—"gone dark," as the islanders said. A great wave of depression rolled over me as I thought about the neighbor who had welcomed me; how glad she was to see, finally, a house reversing the trend toward darkness.

Tylerton, you see, is dying, and perhaps the rest of Smith Island too. I do not even like to put those words down, but statistics compel it. In 1980 the Chesapeake Bay Foundation, my employer on the island, had done a census of the town, and there were 157 people. I updated it in 1987, and there were 124. By 1995, the year-round population was hovering around 80. The whole island, listed in the U.S. 1980 Census at around 675 (somewhat overstated, the preacher at the time thought), is closer to 400 today.

Old people are dying, ten in Tylerton alone within a recent five-year period; and only one baby was born on Tylerton (and five on the island) in that time. Teenage boys are still trying to make it on the water, although more than ever are eyeing jobs with the State Police, or as guards at the new maximum security prison on the Somerset County mainland. Teenage girls seem to have no such conflicts and are leaving. They feel there must be more to life than marriage to a waterman, than picking crabs and cooking and cleaning house and raising kids with limited access to shopping and night life.

Ten percent of Tylerton's population are bachelors. An island mother once interrupted my conversation about worrisome trends in seafood abundance in the bay. The Lord would take care of rockfish and oysters. What worried her was this: "Who's goin' to be left for my son to marry?"

I FELT MORE AND MORE FRUSTRATED about Smith Island's future during our last few months on the island. Tylerton seemed at the point that even two or three more families' leaving could doom the place as a viable community. One day I got a new map of Smith Island and the bay for the education center: a LandSat image that showed the whole watershed from space in astounding detail. On it, you could cover Smith Island with your thumb; and among this thumbprint of marsh, smaller than grains of rice, were three slivers of white, signifying the precious high ground to which clung Ewell, Tylerton, and Rhodes Point.

They were so inconsequential, droplets in an ocean, and yet . . . I got out an old interview I had done years before with Russell Schweikart, the astronaut. Like others who had taken the dramatic step of leaving earth, his altered perspective of the planet had evoked deep emotions: "*. . . you realize that little blue and white thing is everything that means anything to you . . . all of history and music and poetry and art and war and death and birth and love, tears, joy, games, all of it is on that little spot out there that you can cover with your thumb. . . .*"

This book is a quest for the spirit of Smith Island, an attempt to give voice to a people whose eloquence lies simply in their three centuries of working and being here against all odds. A Chesapeake poet, the late Gilbert Byron, once called such fishermen "the greatest poets/who never wrote a line." Their lives are essayed in a fluid environment, inscribed on the hidden bottoms of grassy shallows and oyster beds. Each day, though they have been at it for centuries, the slate is wiped clean; and in a day my children may live to see, as global warming proceeds to raise the level of the oceans, the waters may close atop Smith Island, erasing all physical evidence that the poetry ever existed.

TOM HORTON | 235

WHEN OUR FAMILY LEFT SMITH ISLAND in 1989, the Bay Foundation held a pig roast for us and most of the town came. It was a fun day, long on eating, short on speeches. Many people seemed down, "out of heart," as they would put it. There had been five funerals in recent months, and in a place that close, even one death hits everyone hard. There were more summer people around than I had ever remembered. As more homes go dark, news of their relatively cheap prices is getting around as far away as New York. The "outsiders" who buy them have been, on the whole, nice people. A few single ladies from cities sought the place because they heard it was actually safe to walk anywhere at night and leave your door unlocked. All of them think Tylerton charming, and hope it doesn't ever change; but more and more you hear lawn mowers and power tools going on the Sabbath, and see people strolling in the streets, beers in hand, unmindful or uncaring of the local taboo on public drinking. Some holiday weekends now, for the first time in their long history, islanders wonder whether the place is theirs any more.

We had closed up the old house weeks before, when we put all our belongings on a 48-foot workboat and took them forty miles up Tangier Sound to the headwaters of the Wicomico River where our new home would be. At the pig roast, one of the new educators for the Bay Foundation came up and told me someone had left a light on in the house. It had been burning day and night now for some time. Did I want him to turn it off? I knew about the light, I said. I know you are preaching energy conservation to the groups that come, but please, let it burn a while longer.

Lucille Clifton

the mississippi river
empties into the gulf

and the gulf enters the sea and so forth,
none of them emptying anything,
all of them carrying yesterday
forever on their white tipped backs,
all of them dragging forward tomorrow.
it is the great circulation
of the earth's body, like the blood
of the gods, this river in which the past
is always flowing. every water
is the same water coming round.
everyday someone is standing on the edge
of this river, staring into time,
whispering mistakenly:
only here. only now.

Amy Hempel

In the Cemetery
Where Al Jolson Is Buried

"Tell me things I won't mind forgetting," she said. "Make it useless stuff or skip it."

I began. I told her insects fly through rain, missing every drop, never getting wet. I told her no one in America owned a tape recorder before Bing Crosby did. I told her the shape of the moon is like a banana—you see it looking full, you're seeing it end-on.

The camera made me self-conscious and I stopped. It was trained on us from a ceiling mount—the kind of camera banks use to photograph robbers. It played us to the nurses down the hall in Intensive Care.

"Go on, girl," she said. "You get used to it."

I had my audience. I went on. Did she know that Tammy Wynette had changed her tune? Really. That now she sings "Stand by Your *Friends*"? That Paul Anka did it too, I said. Does "You're Having *Our* Baby." That he got sick of all that feminist bitching.

"What else?" she said. "Have you got something else?"

Oh, yes.

For her I would always have something else.

"Did you know that when they taught the first chimp to talk, it lied? That when they asked her who did it on the desk, she signed back the name of the janitor. And that when they pressed her, she said she was sorry, that it was really the project director. But she was a mother, so I guess she had her reasons."

"Oh, that's good," she said. "A parable."

"There's more about the chimp," I said. "But it will break your heart."

"No, thanks," she says, and scratches at her mask.

WE LOOK LIKE GOOD-GUY OUTLAWS. Good or bad, I am not used to the mask yet. I keep touching the warm spot where my breath, thank God, comes out. She is used to hers. She only ties the strings on top. The other ones—a pro by now—she lets hang loose.

We call this place the Marcus Welby Hospital. It's the white one with the palm trees under the opening credits of all those shows. A Hollywood hospital, though in fact it is several miles west. Off camera, there is a beach across the street.

SHE INTRODUCES ME to a nurse as the Best Friend. The impersonal article is more intimate. It tells me that *they* are intimate, the nurse and my friend.

"I was telling her we used to drink Canada Dry ginger ale and pretend we were in Canada."

"That's how dumb we were," I say.

"You could be sisters," the nurse says.

So how come, I'll bet they are wondering, it took me so long to get to such a glamorous place? But do they ask?

They do not ask.

Two months, and how long is the drive?

The best I can explain it is this—I have a friend who worked one summer in a mortuary. He used to tell me stories. The one that really got to me was not the grisliest, but it's the one that did. A man wrecked his car on 101 going south. He did not lose consciousness. But his arm was taken down to the wet bone—and when he looked at it—it scared him to death.

I mean, he died.

So I hadn't dared to look any closer. But now I'm doing it—and hoping that I will live through it.

SHE SHAKES OUT a summer-weight blanket, showing a leg you did not want to see. Except for that, you look at her and understand the law that requires *two* people to be with the body at all times.

"I thought of something," she says. "I thought of it last night. I think there is a real and present need here. You know," she says, "like for someone to do it for you when you can't do it yourself. You call them up whenever you want—like when push comes to shove."

She grabs the bedside phone and loops the cord around her neck.

"Hey," she says, "the end o' the line."

She keeps on, giddy with something. But I don't know with what.

"I can't remember," she says. "What does Kübler-Ross say comes after Denial?"

It seems to me Anger must be next. Then Bargaining, Depression, and so on and so forth. But I keep my guesses to myself.

"The only thing is," she says, "is where's Resurrection? God knows, I want to do it by the book. But she left out Resurrection."

SHE LAUGHS, and I cling to the sound the way someone dangling above a ravine holds fast to the thrown rope.

"Tell me," she says, "about that chimp with the talking hands. What do they do when the thing ends and the chimp says, 'I don't want to go back to the zoo'?"

When I don't say anything, she says, "Okay—then tell me another animal story. I like animal stories. But not a sick one—I don't want to know about all the seeing-eye dogs going blind."

No, I would not tell her a sick one.

"How about the hearing-ear dogs?" I say. "They're not going deaf, but they are getting very judgmental. For instance, there's this golden retriever in New Jersey, he wakes up the deaf mother and drags her into the daughter's room because the kid has got a flashlight and is reading under the covers."

"Oh, you're killing me," she says. "Yes, you're definitely killing me."

"They say the smart dog obeys, but the smarter dog knows when to disobey."

"Yes," she says, "the smarter anything knows when to disobey. Now, for example."

SHE IS FLIRTING WITH THE GOOD DOCTOR, who has just appeared. Unlike the Bad Doctor, who checks the IV drip before saying good morning, the Good Doctor says things like "God didn't give epileptics a fair shake." The Good Doctor awards himself points for the cripples he could have hit in the parking lot. Because the Good Doctor is a little in love with her, he says maybe a year. He pulls a chair up to her bed and suggests I might like to spend an hour on the beach.

"Bring me something back," she says. "Anything from the beach. Or the gift shop. Taste is no object."

He draws the curtain around her bed.

"Wait!" she cries.

I look in at her.

"Anything," she says, "except a magazine subscription."

The doctor turns away.

I watch her mouth laugh.

WHAT SEEMS DANGEROUS often is not—black snakes, for example, or clear-air turbulence. While things that just lie there, like this beach, are loaded with jeopardy. A yellow dust rising from the ground, the heat that ripens melons overnight—this is earthquake weather. You can sit here braiding the fringe on your towel and the sand will all of a sudden suck down like an hourglass. The air roars. In the cheap apartments on-shore, bathtubs fill themselves and gardens roll up and over like green waves. If nothing happens, the dust will drift and the heat deepen till fear turns to desire. Nerves like that are only bought off by catastrophe.

"IT NEVER HAPPENS when you're thinking about it," she once observed. "Earthquake, earthquake, earthquake," she said.

"Earthquake, earthquake, earthquake," I said.

Like the aviaphobe who keeps the plane aloft with prayer, we kept it up until an aftershock cracked the ceiling.

That was after the big one in seventy-two. We were in college; our dormitory was five miles from the epicenter. When the ride was over and my jabbering pulse began to slow, she served five parts champagne to one part orange juice, and joked about living in Ocean View, Kansas. I offered to drive her to Hawaii on the new world psychics predicted would surface the next time, or the next.

I could not say that now—next.

Whose next? she could ask.

WAS I THE ONLY ONE who noticed that the experts had stopped saying *if* and now spoke of *when?* Of course not; the fearful ran to thousands. We watched the traffic of Japanese beetles for deviation. Deviation might mean more natural violence.

I wanted her to be afraid with me. But she said, "I don't know. I'm just not."

She was afraid of nothing, not even of flying.

I have this dream before a flight where we buckle in and the plane moves down the runway. It takes off at thirty-five miles an hour, and then we're airborne, skimming the tree tops. Still, we arrive in New York on time.

It is so pleasant.

One night I flew to Moscow this way.

SHE FLEW WITH ME ONCE. That time she flew with me she ate macadamia nuts while the wings bounced. She knows the wing tips can bend thirty feet up and thirty feet down without coming off. She believes it. She trusts the laws of aerodynamics. My mind stampedes. I can almost accept that a battleship floats when everybody knows steel sinks.

I see fear in her now, and am not going to try to talk her out of it. She is right to be afraid.

After a quake, the six o'clock news airs a film clip of first-graders yelling at the broken playground per their teacher's instructions.

"*Bad* earth!" they shout, because anger is stronger than fear.

───────────

BUT THE BEACH IS STANDING STILL today. Everyone on it is tranquilized, numb, or asleep. Teenaged girls rub coconut oil on each other's hard-to-reach places. They smell like macaroons. They pry open compacts like clamshells; mirrors catch the sun and throw a spray of white rays across glazed shoulders. The girls arrange their wet hair with silk flowers the way they learned in *Seventeen*. They pose.

A formation of low-riders pulls over to watch with a six-pack. They get vocal when the girls check their tan lines. When the beer is gone, so are they—flexing their cars on up the boulevard.

Above this aggressive health are the twin wrought-iron terraces, painted flamingo pink, of the Palm Royale. Someone dies there every time the sheets are changed. There's an ambulance in the driveway, so the remaining residents line the balconies, rocking and not talking, one-upped.

The ocean they stare at is dangerous, and not just the undertow. You can almost see the slapping tails of sand sharks keeping cruising bodies alive.

If she looked, she could see this, some of it, from her window. She would be the first to say how little it takes to make a thing all wrong.

THERE WAS A SECOND BED in the room when I got back to it!

For two beats I didn't get it. Then it hit me like an open coffin.

She wants every minute, I thought. She wants my life.

"You missed Gussie," she said.

Gussie is her parents' three-hundred-pound narcoleptic maid. Her attacks often come at the ironing board. The pillowcases in that family are all bordered with scorch.

"It's a hard trip for her," I said. "How is she?"

"Well, she didn't fall asleep, if that's what you mean. Gussie's great—

you know what she said? She said, 'Darlin', stop this worriation. Just keep prayin', down on your knees'—me, who can't even get out of bed."

She shrugged. "What am I missing?"

"It's earthquake weather," I told her.

"The best thing to do about earthquakes," she said, "is not to live in California."

"That's useful," I said. "You sound like Reverend Ike—'The best thing to do for the poor is not to be one of them.'"

We're crazy about Reverend Ike.

I noticed her face was bloated.

"You know," she said, "I feel like hell. I'm about to stop having fun."

"The ancients have a saying," I said. "'There are times when the wolves are silent; there are times when the moon howls.'"

"What's that, Navaho?"

"Palm Royale lobby graffiti," I said. "I bought a paper there. I'll read you something."

"Even though I care about nothing?"

I turned to the page with the trivia column. I said, "Did you know the more shrimp flamingo birds eat, the pinker their feathers get?" I said, "Did you know that Eskimos need refrigerators? Do you know *why* Eskimos need refrigerators? Did you know that Eskimos need refrigerators because how else would they keep their food from freezing?"

I turned to page three, to a UPI filler datelined Mexico City. I read her MAN ROBS BANK WITH CHICKEN, about a man who bought a barbecued chicken at a stand down the block from a bank. Passing the bank, he got the idea. He walked in and approached a teller. He pointed the brown paper bag at her and she handed over the day's receipts. It was the smell of barbecue sauce that eventually led to his capture.

THE STORY HAD MADE HER HUNGRY, she said—so I took the elevator down six floors to the cafeteria, and brought back all the ice cream she wanted. We lay side by side, adjustable beds cranked up for optimal TV-viewing, littering the sheets with Good Humor wrappers, picking toasted almonds out of the gauze. We were Lucy and Ethel, Mary and Rhoda in extremis. The blinds were closed to keep light off the screen.

We watched a movie starring men we used to think we wanted to sleep with. Hers was a tough cop out to stop mine, a vicious rapist who went after cocktail waitresses.

"This is a good movie," she said when snipers felled them both.

I missed her already.

A FILIPINO NURSE tiptoed in and gave her an injection. The nurse removed the pile of popsicle sticks from the nightstand—enough to splint a small animal.

The injection made us both sleepy. We slept.

I dreamed she was a decorator, come to furnish my house. She worked in secret, singing to herself. When she finished, she guided me proudly to the door. "How do you like it?" she asked, easing me inside.

Every beam and sill and shelf and knob was draped in gay bunting, with streamers of pastel crepe looped around bright mirrors.

"I HAVE TO GO HOME," I said when she woke up.

She thought I meant home to her house in the Canyon, and I had to say No, *home* home. I twisted my hands in the time-honored fashion of people in pain. I was supposed to offer something. The Best Friend. I could not even offer to come back.

I felt weak and small and failed.

Also exhilarated.

I had a convertible in the parking lot. Once out of that room, I would drive it too fast down the Coast highway through the crab-smelling air. A stop in Malibu for sangria. The music in the place would be sexy and loud. They'd serve papaya and shrimp and watermelon ice. After dinner I would shimmer with lust, buzz with heat, vibrate with life, and stay up all night.

WITHOUT A WORD, she yanked off her mask and threw it on the floor. She kicked at the blankets and moved to the door. She must have hated having to pause for breath and balance before slamming out of Isolation, and out of the second room, the one where you scrub and tie on the white masks.

A voice shouted her name in alarm, and people ran down the corridor. The Good Doctor was paged over the intercom. I opened the door and the nurses at the station stared hard, as if this flight had been my idea.

"Where is she?" I asked, and they nodded to the supply closet.

I looked in. Two nurses were kneeling beside her on the floor, talking to her in low voices. One held a mask over her nose and mouth, the other rubbed her back in slow circles. The nurses glanced up to see if I was the doctor—and when I wasn't, they went back to what they were doing.

"There, there, honey," they cooed.

ON THE MORNING she was moved to the cemetery, the one where Al Jolson is buried, I enrolled in a "Fear of Flying" class. "What is your worst fear?" the instructor asked, and I answered, "That I will finish this course and still be afraid."

I SLEEP WITH A GLASS OF WATER on the nightstand so I can see by its level if the coastal earth is trembling or if the shaking is still me.

WHAT DO I REMEMBER?

I remember only the useless things I hear—that Bob Dylan's mother invented Wite-Out, that twenty-three people must be in a room before there is a fifty-fifty chance two will have the same birthday. Who cares whether or not it's true? In my head there are bath towels swaddling this stuff. Nothing else seeps through.

I review those things that will figure in the retelling: a kiss through surgical gauze, the pale hand correcting the position of the wig. I noted these gestures as they happened, not in any retrospect— though I don't know why looking back should show us more than looking *at*.

It is just possible I will say I stayed the night.

And who is there that can say that I did not?

I THINK OF THE CHIMP, the one with the talking hands.

In the course of the experiment, that chimp had a baby. Imagine how her trainers must have thrilled when the mother, without prompting, began to sign to her newborn.

Baby, drink milk.

Baby, play ball.

And when the baby died, the mother stood over the body, her wrinkled hands moving with animal grace, forming again and again the words: Baby, come hug, Baby, come hug, fluent now in the language of grief.

for Jessica Wolfson

Ralph Angel

Where All the Streets Lead to the Sea

Where all the streets lead to the sea, and full-throated
canaries are free in their cages, and geraniums
splash deeply the shadows of buildings,
in those tiny, dark cages, a woman is singing from her balcony.

With her eyes closed, her voice is a prayer an old
widow is mouthing on the steps of the shuttered
cathedral, syllable by syllable, to the knot in her beads.

In that very pocket, every pocket, where the alleys,
where a man falls into himself and rises up and knows from the inside
the unbearable weight of a white suit,
the black boot polish in his hair threading slowly his cheek.

Whatever got scared
really is scared, that same child who
won't go to sleep because she can't comprehend how it might not

pull her under. Without her. Lost track of.
The one who coughs and with his hand pushes the air away
and coughs again. Those who bring sticks, pieces of broken-down
furniture, a door for the huge, flowering bonfires.

The thousands, walking. More or less sad. More or less
unaccommodated. The woman who in her granddaughter
scrunching her nose like that, tilting her head that way,

discovers again her own mother. And those two,
who got close, with their clothes on fire, it's *their* laughter
crashing onto the damp sand,
roaring.

The Editor

Kay Holloway

Aleda Shirley is the author of two collections of poems, *Long Distance* (University of Miami Press, 1996) and *Chinese Architecture* (University of Georgia Press, 1986). She lives in Jackson, Mississippi.

Contributors

Jennifer Ackerman's *Notes from the Shore* is a personal exploration of the natural life found at the sea's edge. She is writing a second book, *The Longest Thread*, about the biological kinship of humans and other species.

Ralph Angel is the author of *Neither World*, from Miami University Press in 1995, and *Anxious Latitudes*, from Wesleyan University Press in 1986.

Emma Aprile is a poet who lives in Louisville, Kentucky.

Sallie Bingham is a novelist, playwright, and poet. Her latest novel, *Straight Man*, was published in 1996 by Zoland Books, Inc.

Peter Cameron is the author of the novels *Leap Year, The Weekend,* and *Andorra,* and the short story collection, *The Half You Don't Know,* and *One Way or Another.*

Lucille Clifton is the author of *The Terrible Stories* and *Quilting* (BOA Editions, 1996 and 1991), *The Book of Light* (Copper Canyon Press, 1994), and *Ten Oxherding Poems* (Moving Parts Press, 1988).

Charles D'Ambrosio, Jr. is the author of *The Point and Other Stories* and is completing work on a novel for Knopf entitled *Train I Ride.*

Maria Flook is the author of *Reckless Wedding* from Houghton Mifflin (1982), *Sea Room* from Wesleyan University Press (1990), and the following books from Pantheon: *Family Night* (1993), *Open Water* (1995), and *You Have the Wrong Man* (1996).

Terri Ford received grants from both the Kentucky Arts Council and the Kentucky Foundation for Women in 1995. She is a 1984 graduate of the MFA Writing Program at Warren Wilson College, a redhead, coordinates a reading series in Newport, Kentucky, and retains a total spice rack.

Debora Greger is the author of *Movable Islands* (1980), *And* (1985), *The 1002nd Night* (1990), *Off-Season at the Edge of the World* (1994), and *Desert Fathers, Uranium Daughters* (1996). She teaches in the creative writing program at the University of Florida.

Kathleen Halme's first poetry collection, *Every Substance Clothed,* was winner of the 1995 University of Georgia Press Contemporary Poetry Series and the Balcones Poetry Prize. Her newest collection, *Equipoise,* was published by Sarabande Books in 1998. A recipient of a 1997 National Endowment for the Arts fellowship in poetry, Halme is Associate Professor of English at Western Washington University in Bellingham.

James Harms is the author of two collections of poetry, *Modern Ocean* and *The Joy Addict,* both from Carnegie Mellon Press. He directs the creative writing program at West Virginia University.

Robert Hass's most recent book of poems is *Sun Under Wood* (Ecco Press). He teaches at the University of California at Berkeley.

Amy Hempel is the author of three collections of stories, *Reasons to Live, At the Gates of the Animal Kingdom,* and *Tumble Home.* She teaches in the Graduate Writing Seminars at Bennington College, and lives in New York City.

Jane Hirshfield's most recent books are *The Lives of the Heart* (poetry) and *Nine Gates: Entering the Mind of Poetry,* both published by HarperCollins in 1997. She has received a Guggenheim Fellowship, The Bay Area Book Reviewers Award, The Poetry Center Book Award, and other honors.

Tom Horton, environmental columnist for the *Baltimore Sun* and author of five books about the Chesapeake Bay, lives in Hebron, Maryland.

Gray Jacobik's collection of poetry, *The Double Task,* received the Juniper Prize for 1997. She teaches literature at Eastern Connecticut State University and lives in Pomfret, Connecticut.

Mark Jarman's latest collection of poetry is *Questions for Ecclesiastes.* He is co-editor of *Rebel Angels: 25 Poets of the New Formalism* and co-author of *The Reaper Essays.* He teaches at Vanderbilt University.

Yusef Komunyakaa's recent books of poems are *Thieves of Paradise* (Wesleyan University Press) and *Trickster's Confession,* a bilingual edition (Ediciones El Tucan de Virginia). He teaches at Princeton University.

Li-Young Lee was born in 1957, in Jakarta, Indonesia. Presently, he is living in Chicago, Illinois, with his wife and two sons. He is the author of *Rose* (1986) and *The City in Which I Love You* (1990), both from BOA Editions.

Peter Matthiessen was born in New York City in 1927 and had already begun his writing career by the time he graduated from Yale University in 1950. The following year, he was a founder of *The Paris Review*. Besides *At Play in the Fields of the Lord*, which was nominated for the National Book Award, he has published six other works of fiction, including *Far Tortuga*, *Killing Mr. Watson*, and *Lost Man's River*. Mr. Matthiessen's parallel career as a naturalist and explorer has resulted in numerous widely acclaimed books of nonfiction, among them *The Tree Where Man Was Born*, which was nominated for the National Book Award, and *The Snow Leopard*, which won it.

Shara McCallum's poems have been published in numerous journals, including *The Iowa Review*, *The Antioch Review*, *Chelsea*, *Another Chicago Magazine*, *Senecca Review*, and *Quarterly West*.

Kristina McGrath's first novel *House Work* was published in 1994 and selected by the *New York Times* as a Notable Book of the Year. She is a recipient of grants in poetry and fiction from the New York Foundation for the Arts, a fiction grant from the Kentucky Foundation for Women, a Kenyon Review Award for Literary Excellence in Fiction, a Pushcart, and a Writer's Voice Residency Award.

Susan Minot is the author of the novels *Evening*, *Monkeys* and *Folly*, as well as the collection *Lust & Other Stories*. Her work has been published in a dozen countries. She lives in New York City.

Carol Muske's new books are *An Octave above Thunder, New and Selected Poems* from Penguin (1997) and *Women and Poetry* from the

University of Michigan Press (1997). She teaches English and Creative Writing at the University of South Carolina.

Mark Richard's first collection of stories, *The Ice at the Bottom of the World* (Alfred A. Knopf, 1989), received the Pen/Hemingway Award. His novel, *Fishboy*, was published by Doubleday in 1993. *Charity*, his second story collection, was published by Doubleday/Nan A. Talese in 1998. He has received the Whiting Foundation Writers' Award and the Hobson Prize, as well as fellowships from the National Endowment for the Arts and the New York Foundation for the Arts. He is a correspondent for BBC radio.

David St. John's *Study for the World's Body: New and Selected Poems* (HarperCollins, 1994) was nominated for the National Book Award in Poetry.

Chase Twichell is the author of *The Ghost of Eden* (Ontario Review Press, 1995), *Perdido* (Farrar, Straus & Giroux, 1991), *The Odds*, and *Northern Spy* (University of Pittsburgh Press, 1986 and 1981).

Michael Waters teaches at Salisbury State University on the Eastern Shore of Maryland. His six books of poetry include *Green Ash, Red Maple, Black Gum* (BOA Editions, 1997) and *Bountiful* (Carnegie Mellon University Press, 1992). BOA will publish his *New and Selected* in 2000.

David Wojahn is the author of five collections of poetry, most recently *The Falling Hour* (1997) and *Late Empire* (1994), both published by the University of Pittsburgh Press. He teaches at Indiana University and in the MFA Writing Program of Vermont College.

Acknowledgments

Jennifer Ackerman. "Osprey" is reprinted from *Notes from the Shore,* © 1995 by Jennifer Ackerman. Reprinted by permission of Viking Penguin, a division of Penguin Books USA Inc.

Ralph Angel. "Where All the Streets Lead to the Sea" is reprinted from *Neither World,* © 1995 by Ralph Angel. Reprinted by permission of the author.

Emma Aprile. "Hawaii" appears here for the first time. Used by permission of the author.

Sallie Bingham. "Off-Season" appears here for the first time. Used by permission of the author.

Peter Cameron. "Nuptials & Heathens" is reprinted from *One Way or Another,* © 1986 by Peter Cameron, published by Harper & Row Publishers. Reprinted by permission of the author.

Lucille Clifton. "the mississippi river empties into the gulf" is reprinted from *The Terrible Stories,* © 1996 by Lucille Clifton. Reprinted by permission of BOA Editions, Ltd., 260 East Ave., Rochester, NY 14604.

Robert Hass. "On the Coast near Sausalito" is reprinted from *Field Guide*, © 1973 by Robert Hass. Reprinted by permission of Yale University Press.

Amy Hempel. "In the Cemetery Where Al Jolson Is Buried" is reprinted from *Reasons to Live*, © 1985 by Amy Hempel, published by Alfred A. Knopf, Inc. Reprinted by permission of the author.

Jane Hirshfield. "Just Below the Surface" is reprinted from *October Palace*, © 1994 by Jane Hirshfield. Reprinted by permission of HarperCollins Publishers.

Tom Horton. "The Greatest Poets" is reprinted from *An Island Out of Time*, © 1996 by Tom Horton. Reprinted by permission of W.W. Norton & Company, Inc.

Gray Jacobik. "Sandwoman" first appeared in *Southern Poetry Review*; "Heat Wave" first appeared in *Confrontation*. Used by permission of the author.

Mark Jarman. "Wave" and "Skin Cancer" are reprinted from *Questions for Ecclesiastes*, © 1997 by Mark Jarman. Reprinted by permission of Story Line Press.

Yusef Komunyakaa. "Newport Beach, 1979" is reprinted from *Copacetic*, © 1984 by Yusef Komunyakaa. "Boat People" is reprinted from *Dien Cai Dau*, © 1988 by Yusef Komunyakaa. Both books were published by Wesleyan University Press. The poems are reprinted by permission of University Press of New England.

David St. John. "The Shore" and "The Reef" are reprinted from *Study for the World's Body: New and Selected Poems*, published by HarperCollins, © 1994 by David St. John. Reprinted by permission of the author.

Chase Twichell. "Why All Good Music Is Sad" is reprinted from *Perdido*, © 1991 by Chase Twichell. Reprinted by permission of Farrar, Straus & Giroux, Inc.

Michael Waters. "Driftwood" is reprinted from *Green Ash, Red Maple, Black Gum*, © 1997 by Michael Waters. Reprinted by permission of BOA Editions, Ltd., 260 East Ave., Rochester, NY 14604. "Moray Eels" and "Scotch and Sun" are reprinted from *Bountiful*, published by Carnegie Mellon University Press, © 1992 by Michael Waters. Reprinted by permission of the author. "The Turtles of Santa Rosa" is reprinted from *The Burden Lifters*, published by Carnegie Mellon University Press, © 1989 by Michael Waters. Reprinted by permission of the author.

David Wojahn. "Shadow Girl" is reprinted from *Glassworks*, © 1987 by David Wojahn. Reprinted by permission of the University of Pittsburgh Press.